'A flash in the heavens that makes you look up and believe in miracles... Here, in fresh, graceful prose, is a profound story that dares to be as tender as it is ghastly... I haven't been so overwhelmed by a novel in years. At the risk of raising your expectations too high, I have to say you simply must read this book'
Washington Post

'A powerful tale... Rivals anything Michael Ondaatje has written in its emotional force'
Boston Globe

'Powerful, convincing, beautifully realised – it's hard to believe that *A Constellation of Vital Phenomena* is a first novel. Anthony Marra is a writer to watch and savour'
TC Boyle

'A book of violence and beauty, and the undisputed arrival of a major new talent'
Globe and Mail

'Resembles the Joseph Heller of *Catch-22* and the Jonathan Safran Foer of *Everything Is Illuminated*'
New York Times

'An absolute masterpiece... I can't wait to see what's next for this extraordinarily talented young author'
Sarah Jessica Parker, *Entertainment Weekly*

A Constellation of Vital Phenomena

A Constellation of
Vital Phenomena

ANTHONY MARRA

VINTAGE BOOKS
London

Published by Vintage 2014
First published in the United States of America in 2013 by Hogarth, an
imprint of the Crown Publishing Group, a division of Random House

12

First published in Great Britain in 2013 by
Hogarth, an imprint of Chatto & Windus

Vintage
Random House, 20 Vauxhall Bridge Road,
London SW1V 2SA

www.vintage-books.co.uk

Addresses for companies within The Random House Group Limited
can be found at: www.randomhouse.co.uk/offices

The Random House Group Limited Reg. No. 954009

A CIP catalogue record for this book
is available from the British Library

ISBN 9780099575573

Penguin Random House is committed to a sustainable future for
our business, our readers and our planet. This book is made from
Forest Stewardship Council® certified paper.

Printed and bound in Great Britain by Clays Ltd, Elcograf S.p.A.

Typeset in Walbaum by Palimpsest Book Production Ltd,
Falkirk, Stirlingshire

To my parents and sister

It was of this death that I was reminded by the crushed thistle in the midst of the ploughed field.

– Leo Tolstoy, *Hadji Murád*

The First and Second Days

Chapter 1

1994 1995 1996 1997 1998 1999 2000 2001 2002 2003 2004

ON THE MORNING AFTER THE FEDS BURNED down her house and took her father, Havaa woke from dreams of sea anemones. While the girl dressed, Akhmed, who hadn't slept at all, paced outside the bedroom door, watching the sky brighten on the other side of the window glass; the rising sun had never before made him feel late. When she emerged from the bedroom, looking older than her eight years, he took her suitcase and she followed him out the front door. He had led the girl to the middle of the street before he raised his eyes to what had been her house. 'Havaa, we should go,' he said, but neither moved.

The snow softened around their boots as they stared across the street to the wide patch of flattened ash. A few orange embers hissed in pools of grey snow, but all else was char. Not seven years earlier, Akhmed had helped Dokka build an extension so the girl would have a room of her own. He had drawn the blueprints and chopped the hardwood and cut it into boards and turned them into a room; and when Dokka had promised to help him build an extension to his own house, should he ever have a child, Akhmed had thanked his friend and walked home, the knot in his throat unravelling into a sob when the door closed behind him. Carrying that lumber the forty metres from the forest had left his knuckles blistered, his underarms sopping, but now a few hours of flames had lifted what had taken him months to design, weeks to carry, days to build, all but the nails and rivets, all but the hinges and bolts, all into the sky. And too were carried the small treasures that had made Dokka's house his own. There was the hand-carved chess set on a round side table; when moved, the squat white king wobbled from side to side, like a man just sober enough to stand, and Dokka had named his majesty Boris Yeltsin. There was the porcelain vase adorned with Persian arabesques, and beside that a cassette deck–radio with an antenna long enough to scrape the ceiling when propped up on a telephone book, yet too short to reach anything but static. There was the eighty-five-year-old Qur'an, the purple cover writhing with calligraphy, that Dokka's grandfather had purchased in Mecca. There were these things and the flames ate these things, and since fire doesn't distinguish between the word of God and the word of the Soviet Communications Registry Bureau, both Qur'an and telephone directory returned to His mouth in the same inhalation of smoke.

The girl's fingers braceleted his wrist. He wanted to throw her over his shoulder and sprint northward until the forest swallowed the village, but standing before the blackened timbers, he couldn't summon the strength to bring a consoling word to his lips, to hold the girl's hand in his own, to move his feet in the direction he wanted them to go.

'That's my house.' Her voice broke their silence and he heard it as he would the only sound in an empty corridor.

'Don't think of it like that,' he said.

'Like what?'

'Like it's still yours.'

He wound her bright orange scarf around her neck and frowned at the sooty fingerprint on her cheek. He had been awake in bed the previous night when the Feds came. First the murmur of a diesel engine, a low rumble he'd come to fear more than gunfire, then Russian voices. He had gone to the living room and pulled back the blackout curtain as far as he dared. Through the triangle of glass, headlights parted the night. Four soldiers, stocky, well fed, emerged from the truck. One drank from a vodka bottle and cursed the snow each time he stumbled. This soldier's grandfather had told him, the morning the soldier reported to the Vladivostok conscription centre, that he would have perished in Stalingrad if not for the numbing grace of vodka; the soldier, whose cheeks were divoted from years of applying toothpaste to his adolescent acne, believed Chechnya to be a worse war than Stalingrad, and rationed his vodka accordingly. From his living room Akhmed wanted to shout, beat a drum, set off a flare. But across the street, they had already reached Dokka's door and he didn't even look to the phone that was without a pulse for ten years now. They knocked on the door once, twice, then kicked it down. Through the doorway, Akhmed watched torchlight move across the walls. So passed the longest two minutes of Akhmed's life until the soldiers reappeared in the doorway with Dokka. The gaffer-tape strip across his mouth wrinkled with his muted screams. They pulled a black hood over his head. Where was Havaa? Sweat formed on Akhmed's forehead. His hands felt impossibly heavy. When the soldiers grabbed Dokka by the shoulders and belt, tumbling him into the back of the truck and slamming the door, the relief falling over Akhmed was quickly peeled back by self-loathing, because he was alive, safe in his living room, while in the truck over the road, not twenty metres away, Dokka was a dead man. The designation 'o2' was stencilled above the truck bumper in white paint, meaning it belonged to the Interior Ministry, meaning there would be no record of the arrest, meaning Dokka had never officially been taken, meaning he would never come back. 'Where's the girl?' the soldiers asked one another. 'She's not here.' 'What if she's hiding beneath the floorboards?' 'She's not.' 'Take care of it just in case.' The drunken soldier uncapped a petrol jug and stumbled into Dokka's house; when he returned to the threshold, he tossed a match behind him and closed the door. Flames clawed their way up the front curtains. The glass panes puddled on the sill. Where was Havaa? When the truck finally left, the fire had spread to the walls and roof. Akhmed waited until the tail lights had shrunk to the size of cherries before crossing the street. Running a wide circle around the flames, he entered the forest behind the house. His boots broke the frigid undergrowth and he could have counted the rings of tree stumps by the firelight. Behind the house, hiding among the trees, the girl's face flickered. Streaks of pale skin began under her eyes, striping the ash on her cheeks. 'Havaa,' he called out. She sat on a suitcase and didn't respond to her name. He held her like a bundle of loose sticks in his arms, carried her to his house and with a damp towel wiped the ash from her forehead. He tucked her in bed beside his invalid wife and didn't know what to do next. He could have gone back outside and thrown snowballs at the burning house, or lain in bed so the girl would feel the warmth of two grown bodies, or performed his ablutions and prostrated himself, but he had completed the *isha'a* hours earlier and if five daily prayers hadn't spared Dokka's house, a sixth wouldn't put out the flames. Instead he went to the living-room window, drew open the blackout curtains, and watched the house he had helped build disappear into light. And now, in the morning, as he tightened the orange scarf around her neck, he found a fingerprint on the girl's cheek, and, because it could have been Dokka's, he left it.

'Where are we going?' she asked. She stood in the frozen furrow of the previous night's tyre tracks. The snow stretched on either side. Akhmed hadn't prepared for this. He couldn't imagine why the Feds would want Dokka, much less the girl. She stood no taller than his stomach and weighed no more than a basket of firewood, but to Akhmed she seemed an immense and overwhelming creature whom he was destined to fail.

'We're going to the city hospital,' he said, with what he hoped was an assertive tone.

'Why?'

'Because the hospital is safe. It's where people go when they need help. And I know someone there, another doctor,' he said, though all he knew of her was her name. 'She'll help.'

'How?'

'I'm going to ask if you can stay with her.' What was he saying? Like most of his plans, this one seemed so robust in his mind but fell like a flightless bird when released to the air. The girl frowned.

'He's not coming back, is he?' she asked. She focused on the blue leather suitcase that sat on the street between them. Eight months earlier, her father had asked her to prepare the suitcase and leave it in the cupboard, where it had remained until the previous night, when he thrust it into her hands and pushed her out the back door as the Feds broke through the front.

'I don't think so.'

'But you don't know?' It wasn't an accusation, but he took

7

it as one. Was he so incompetent a physician that she hesitated to trust him with her father's life even in speculation? 'We should be safe,' he said. 'It's safer to think he won't come back.'

'But what if he does?'

The longing knotted into such a simple question was more than he could contemplate. What if she cried? It suddenly seemed like a terrifying possibility. How would he stop her? He had to keep her calm, keep himself calm; panic, he knew, could spread between two people more quickly than any virus. He fiddled with her scarf. Somehow it had survived the fire as orange as the day it was pulled from the dye. 'How about this: if he comes back, I'll tell him where you are. Is that a good idea?'

'My father is a good idea.'

'Yes, he is,' Akhmed said, relieved they had this to agree on.

They plodded along the Eldár Forest Service Road, the village's main thoroughfare, and their footprints began where the tyre tracks ended. On either side he saw houses by surname rather than address. A face appeared and vanished in an unboarded window.

'Pull your headscarf tighter,' he instructed. But for his years at medical school, he had spent his whole life in Eldár and no longer trusted the traditional clan system of *teips* that had survived a century of Tsarist rule, then a century of Soviet rule, only to dissolve in a war of national independence. Reincarnated in 1999, after a truce too lawless to be called peace, the war had frayed the village *teip* into lesser units of loyalty until all but the fidelity of a parent for a child wore thin enough to break. Logging, the village's sole stable industry, had ceased soon after the first bombs fell, and without viable prospects those who couldn't emigrate ran guns for the rebels or informed for the Feds to survive.

He wrapped his arm around Havaa's shoulder as they walked. The girl had always been strong and stoic, but this resignation, this passivity, was something else. She clomped along, kicking snow with each footstep, and in an attempt to cheer her Akhmed whispered a joke about a blind imam and a deaf prostitute, a joke that really wasn't appropriate for an eight-year-old, but was the only one Akhmed could remember. She didn't smile, but was listening. She zipped her puffy jacket over a sweatshirt that in Manchester, England, had warmed the shoulders of five brothers before the sixth, a staunchly philanthropic six-year-old, had given it to his school's Red Cross donation so his mother would have to buy him a new one.

At the end of the village, where the forest narrowed on the road, they passed a metre-tall portrait nailed to a tree trunk. Two years earlier, after forty-one of the villagers had disappeared in a single day, Akhmed had drawn their forty-one portraits on forty-one plywood boards, weatherproofed them, and hung them throughout the village. This one was of a beautiful, self-admiring woman whose second daughter he had delivered. Despite his hounding her for years, she never had paid him for the delivery. After she was abducted, he had decided to draw on her portrait a single hair curling from her left nostril. He had grinned at the vain woman's ghost and then made peace with it. She looked like a beheaded giantess staring from the trunk. Soon she was no more than two eyes, a nose and a mouth fading between the trees.

The forest rose around them, tall skeletal birches, grey coils of bark unravelling from the trunks. They walked on the side of the road, where frozen undergrowth expanded across the gravel. Here, beyond the trails of tank treads, the chances of stepping on a landmine diminished. Still he watched for rises in the frost. He walked a few metres ahead of the girl, just in case. He remembered another joke, this one about a lovesick commissar, but decided not to tell it. When she began straggling, he led her five minutes into the woods to a felled log unseen from the road. As they sat down, she asked for her blue suitcase. He gave it to her and she opened it, taking a silent inventory of its contents.

'What's in there?' he asked.

'My souvenirs,' she said, but he didn't know what she meant. He unwrapped a hunk of dry black bread from a white handkerchief, split it in two uneven pieces, and gave her the larger one. She ate quickly. Hunger was a sensation so long situated in his abdomen he felt it as he would an inflamed organ. He took his time, tonguing the pulp into a little oval and resting it against his cheek like a lozenge. If the bread wouldn't fill his stomach, it might at least fill his mouth. The girl had finished half of hers before he took a second bite.

'You shouldn't rush,' he said. 'There are no taste buds in your stomach.'

She paused to consider his reasoning, then took another bite. 'There's no hunger in your tongue,' she mumbled between chews. Her cupped hand caught the crumbs and tossed them back in her mouth.

'I used to hate black bread,' he said. When he was a child he would only eat black bread if it was slathered in a spoonful of honey. Over the course of a year, his mother weaned him from it by slicing larger pieces, until his breakfast consisted of a small, sad oasis of honey on a desert of black bread.

'Can I have yours, then?'

'I said used to,' he said, and imagined a brimming jar of

honey, standing on a worktop without a breadboard in sight.

She dropped to her knees and examined the underside of the log. 'Will Ula be all right alone?' she asked.

His wife wasn't all right alone, with him, with anyone. He believed she had, in technical terms, lupus coupled with early-onset dementia, but in practice her nerves were so criss-crossed that her elbows ached when she spoke and her left foot had more sense than her brain. Before leaving that morning he had told Ula he would be gone for the day. As she gazed at him through her blank daze, he felt himself as one of her many visions, and he held her hand, and described from memory the placid pasture of a Zakharov oil painting, the herb garden and the cottage, until she fell back asleep. When she woke again that morning would she still see him sitting on the bed beside her? Perhaps part of him was still there, sitting on the bed; perhaps he was something she had dreamed up.

'She's an adult,' he said at last and without much thought. 'You don't need to worry about adults.'

Behind the log, Havaa didn't reply.

He had always tried to treat Havaa as a child and she always went along with it, as though childhood and innocence were fantastical creatures that had died long ago, resurrected only in games of make-believe. The only times she had been in a schoolhouse were when they went to steal child-sized desks for firewood, but sometimes he imagined they shared what was essentially the same wisdom separated by years and experience. It wasn't true, of course, but he had to believe that she had lived beyond her years, that she could confront what no eight-year-old is capable of confronting. She climbed from the log without looking at him.

'What's that?' he asked. She carefully lifted a yellow shape from her palm.

'A frozen insect,' she said, and put it in her coat pocket.

'In case you get hungry later?' he asked.

She smiled for the first time that day.

They trod along the edge of the road and the girl's quickened pace compensated for their stop. With deep breaths he tried to unweave threads of diesel fumes or burning rubber from the air. The daylight provided a degree of safety. They wouldn't be mistaken for wild dogs.

They heard the soldiers before the checkpoint came in sight. Akhmed raised his hand. Wind filled the spaces between his fingers. Once used to transport timber, the Eldár Forest Service Road connected the village to the city of Volchansk. The gaps between the tree trunks provided the only exit points between village and city, and in recent months the Feds had reduced their presence to a single checkpoint. It lay another half-kilometre away, at the end of a sharp curve.

'We're going back into the woods.'

'To eat again?'

'Just to walk. We need to be quiet.'

The girl nodded and raised her index finger to her lips. The entire forest had frozen and fallen to the ground. Crooked branches reached through the snow and scratched their shins from every angle as they walked a wide arc around the checkpoint. Visible through the trees, the checkpoint was no more than a wilted army tarpaulin nailed to a poplar trunk in a failed attempt to lend an air of legitimacy. A handful of soldiers stood by it. Crossing the floor of frigid leaves in silence was impossible, but the soldiers, eight men who between them could share more venereal diseases than Chechen words, seemed no more alert than brain-sick bucks, and they returned to the road a quarter-kilometre past the checkpoint. The sun shone yolk-yellow between white clouds. Nearly noon. The trees they passed repeated on and on into the woods. None was remarkable when compared to the next, but each was individual in some small regard: the number of limbs, the girth of trunk, the circumference of shed leaves encircling the base. No more than minor particularities, but minor particularities were what transformed two eyes, a nose and a mouth into a face.

The trees opened to a wide field, bisected by the road.

'Let's walk faster,' he said, and the girl's footsteps hastened behind him. They were nearly halfway across when they came upon the severed hindquarters of a wolf. Further into the field, blood dyed the snow a reddish brown. Nothing had decomposed in the cold. The head and front legs lay exposed on the ground, connected to the wolf's back end by three metres of pulped innards. What was left of the face was frozen in the expression it had died with. The tongue ribboned from its maw.

'It was a careless animal,' Akhmed said. He tried to look away, but there was wolf everywhere. 'It didn't watch for landmines.'

'We're more careful.'

'Yes, we'll stay on the road. We won't walk in the fields.'

She stood close to him. Her shoulder pressed against his side. This was the furthest she'd ever been from home.

'It wasn't always like this,' he said. 'Before you were born there were wolves and birds and insects and goats and bears and sheep and deer.'

The heavy snow stretched a hundred metres to the forest. A few dead stalks rose through the brown frost, where the wolf would lie until spring. With heavy breaths they shaped the air. No prophet had augured this end. Neither the sounding of trumpets nor the beating of seraphic wings had heralded this particular field, with this particular girl, holding his particular hand.

'They were here,' he said, staring into the field.

'Where did the Feds take them?'

'We should keep walking.'

White moths circled a dead light bulb.

A firm hand on her shoulder lifted her from the dream. Sonja lay on a trauma ward hospital bed, still dressed in her scrubs. Before she looked to the hand that had woken her, before she rose from the imprint her body had made in the weak mattress foam, she reached for her pocket, from instinct rather than want, and shook the amber pill bottle as though its contents had followed her into her dreams and also required waking. The amphetamines rattled in reply. She sat up, conscious, blinking away the moth wings.

'There's someone here to see you,' Nurse Deshi announced from behind her, and began stripping the sheets before Sonja stood.

'See me about what?' she asked. She bent to touch her feet, relieved to find them still there.

'Now she thinks I'm a secretary,' the old nurse said, shaking her head. 'Soon she'll start pinching my rump like that oncologist who chased out four secretaries in a year. A shameful profession. I've never met an oncologist who wasn't a hedonist.'

'Deshi, who's here to see me?'

The old nurse looked up, startled. 'A man from Eldár.'

'About Natasha?'

Deshi tensed her lips. She could have said *no* or *not this time* or *it's time to give up*, but instead shook her head.

The man leaned against the corridor wall. A one-size-too-small navy *pes* with beaded tassels roosted on the back

14

of his head. His jacket hung from his shoulders as if still on the hanger. A girl stood beside him, inspecting the contents of a blue suitcase.

'Sofia Andreyevna Rabina?' he asked.

She hesitated. She hadn't heard or spoken her full name aloud in eight years and only answered to her diminutive. 'Call me Sonja,' she said.

'My name is Akhmed.' A short black beard shrouded his cheeks. Shaving cream was an unaffordable luxury for many; she couldn't tell if the man was a Wahhabi insurgent or just poor.

'Are you a bearded one?' she asked.

He reached for his whiskers in embarrassment. 'No, no. Absolutely not. I just haven't shaved recently.'

'What do you want?'

He nodded to the girl. She wore an orange scarf, an oversized pink coat, and a sweatshirt advertising Manchester United, likely, Sonja imagined, from the glut of Manchester apparel that had flooded charity donations after Beckham was traded to Madrid. She had the pale, waxen skin of an unripe pear. When Sonja approached, the girl had raised the lid of the suitcase, slipped her hand inside and held an object hidden from Sonja's view.

'She needs a place to stay,' Akhmed said.

'And I need a plane ticket to the Black Sea.'

'She has nowhere to go.'

'And I haven't had a tan in years.'

'Please,' he said.

'This is a hospital, not an orphanage.'

'There are no orphanages.'

Out of habit she turned to the window, but she saw nothing through the gaffer-taped panes. The only light came from the fluorescent bulbs overhead, whose blue tint made them all appear hypothermic. Was that a moth circling the fixture? No, she was just seeing things again.

'Her father was taken by the security forces last night. To the Landfill, most likely.'

'I'm sorry to hear that.'

'He was a good man. He was an arborist in Eldár Forest before the wars. He didn't have fingers. He was very good at chess.'

'He *is* very good at chess,' the girl snapped, and glared at Akhmed. Grammar was the only place the girl could keep her father alive, and after amending Akhmed's statement, she leaned back against the wall and with small, certain breaths, said '*is is is.*' Her father was the face of her morning and night, he was everything, so saturating Havaa's world that she could no more describe him than she could the air.

Akhmed summoned the arborist with small declarative memories, and Sonja let him go on longer than she otherwise would because she, too, had tried to resurrect by recitation, had tried to recreate the thing by drawing its shape in cinders, and hoped that by compiling lists of Natasha's favourite foods and songs and annoying habits, her sister might spontaneously materialise under the pressure of the particularities.

'I'm sorry,' she repeated.

'The Feds weren't looking for Dokka alone,' he said quietly, glancing to the girl.

'What would they want with her?' she asked.

'What do they want with anyone?' His urgent self-importance was familiar; she'd seen it on the faces of so many husbands, and brothers, and fathers, and sons, and was glad she could see it here, on the face of a stranger, and not feel moved. 'Please let her stay,' he said.

'She can't.' It was the right decision, the responsible one.

Caring for the dying overwhelmed her. She couldn't be expected to care for the living as well.

The man looked to his feet with a disappointed frown that inexplicably resurrected the memory of *b) electrophilic aromatic substitution*, the answer to the only question on her university organic chemistry exam she'd got wrong. 'How many doctors are here?' he asked, apparently deciding to try a different tack.

'One.'

'To run an entire hospital?'

She shrugged. What did he expect? Those with advanced degrees, personal savings and the foresight to flee had done so. 'Deshi runs it. I just work here.'

'I was a GP. Not a surgeon or specialist, but I was licensed.' He raised his hand to his beard. A crumb fell out. 'The girl will stay with you and I will work here until a home is found for her.'

'No one will take her.'

'Then I will keep working here. I graduated from medical school in the top tenth of my class.'

Already this man's habit of converting entreaty to command annoyed her. She had returned from England with her full name eight years earlier and still received the respect that had so surprised her when she first arrived in London to study medicine. It didn't matter that she was both a woman and an ethnic Russian; as the only surgeon in Volchansk, she was revered, honoured and cherished in war as she never would be in peace. And this peasant doctor, this man so thin she could have pushed against his stomach and felt his spine, he expected her acquiescence? Even more than his tone of voice she resented the accuracy of his appraisal. As the last of a staff of five hundred, she was engulfed by the burden of care. She lived on amphetamines and sweetened condensed milk, had regular hallucinations, had difficulty empathising with her patients, and had seen enough cases of secondary traumatic stress disorder to recognise herself among them. At the end of the hall, through the partially opened waiting-room door, she saw the hemline of a black dress, the grey of once-white tennis shoes, and a green hijab that, rather than covering the long black hair, held the broken arm of a young woman who was made of bird bones and calcium deficiency, who believed this to be her twenty-second broken bone, when in fact it was merely her twenty-first.

'The top ten per cent?' Sonja asked with no small amount of scepticism.

Akhmed nodded eagerly. 'Ninety-sixth percentile to be precise.'

'Then tell me, what would you do with an unresponsive patient?'

'Well, hmm, let's see,' Akhmed stammered. 'First I would have him fill out a questionnaire to get a sense of his medical history along with any conditions or diseases that might run in his family.'

'You would give an unconscious, unresponsive patient a questionnaire?'

'Oh, no. Don't be silly,' he said, hesitating. 'I would give the questionnaire to the patient's wife instead.'

Sonja closed her eyes, hoping that when she opened them, this idiot doctor and his ward would have vanished. No luck. 'Do you want to know what I would do?' she asked. 'I would check the airway, then check for breathing, then check for a pulse, then stabilise the cervical spine. Nine times out of ten, I'd be concentrating on haemostasis. I'd be cutting off the patient's clothes to inspect the entire body for wounds.'

'Well, yes,' Akhmed said. 'I would do all of that while the patient's wife was filling out the questionnaire.'

'Let's try something closer to your level. What is this?' she asked, raising her thumb.

'I believe that is a thumb.'

'No,' she said. 'It is the first digit, composed of the metacarpal, the proximal phalange and the distal phalange.'

'That's another way of saying it.'

'And this?' she asked, pointing to her left eye. 'What can you say about this besides the fact that it is my eye, and it is brown and used for seeing?'

He frowned, uncertain what he could add. 'Dilated pupils,' he said at last.

'And did they bother teaching the top ten per cent what dilated pupils are symptomatic of?'

'Head injuries, drug use or sexual arousal.'

'Or more likely because the hallway is poorly lit.' She tapped a small scar on her temple. No one knew where it had come from. 'And this?'

He smiled. 'I have no idea what's going on in there.'

She bit her lip and nodded. 'OK,' she said. 'We need someone to wash dirty sheets anyway. She can stay if you work.' The girl stood behind Akhmed. In her palm a yellow insect lounged in a pool of melting ice. Sonja already regretted her consent. 'What's your name?' she asked in Chechen.

'Havaa,' Akhmed said. He gently pushed the girl towards her. The girl leaned against his palm, afraid to venture beyond its reach.

A year earlier, when Natasha had disappeared for the second and final time, Sonja's one- and two-night stays in the trauma ward had lengthened into weeks. After five weeks had passed since she'd last slid the key into the double lock, she had given up on the idea of ever going back. The twelve blocks to her flat might as well have been the Sahara. Waiting for her there was a silence more terrible than anything she heard on the operating table. Years before that, she had posed with her hand pressed against a distant Big Ben, so that in the photograph her fiancé had taken, she appeared to be holding up the clock tower. He had taken it on the eighth of their seventeen-day engagement. The photograph was taped above the desk in her bedroom, but not even its rescue was enough to lure her home. Living in the trauma ward wasn't much of a change. She'd already been spending seventeen of her eighteen waking hours in the ward. She knew the bodies she opened, fixed and closed more intimately than their spouses or parents did, and that intimacy came as near to creation as the breath of God's first word.

So when she offered to let the girl stay with her, she meant here at the hospital; but the girl already knew that as she followed Sonja to her room.

'This is where we'll sleep, all right?' she said, setting the girl's suitcase by the stacked mattresses. The girl still held the insect. 'Is there something in your hand?' Sonja asked tentatively.

'A dead insect,' the girl said.

Sonja sighed, grateful, at least, to know she wasn't imagining it. 'Why?'

'Because I found it in the forest and brought it with me.'

'Again, why?'

'Because it needs to be buried facing Mecca.'

She closed her eyes. She couldn't begin with this now. Even as a child she had hated children; she still did. 'I'll be back later,' she said, and returned to the corridor.

If nothing else, Akhmed was quick to undress. In the time it took her to show the girl to her room, he had changed into white scrubs. She found him preening before the hallway mirror.

'This is a hospital, not a ballroom,' she said.

'I've never worn scrubs before.' He turned from her, but the mirror held his blush.

'How could you go through training without wearing scrubs?'

He closed his eyes and his blush deepened. 'My professors didn't have much faith in me. I was never, exactly, what you would call a house officer.'

'This isn't what I want to hear right after I take you on.'

'I just feel privileged to work here.' The sleeves showed off his pale biceps. 'I always thought these would be looser.'

'They're women's scrubs.'

'You don't have any for men?'

'No men work here.'

'So I'm wearing women's clothes.'

'You'll need to wear a hijab, too.' His face paled. 'I'm kidding,' she added. 'A headscarf is sufficient.'

He nodded, unconvinced. Clearly, she had hired a buffoon, but a buffoon who could wash linen, make beds and deal with relatives was better than no buffoon at all. 'Have you ever been here before?' she asked, disinclined to give more than a brief tour of the hospital.

'Yes.'

'When?'

'I was born here.'

She took him through the ghost wards: cardiology, internal medicine, endocrinology. A layer of dust and ash recorded their path. 'Where is everything?' he asked. The rooms were empty. Mattresses, sheets, hypodermics, disposable gowns, surgical tape, film dressing, thermometers and IV bags had been moved downstairs. All that remained was bolted to the floor and built into the walls, along with items of no practical use: family portraits, professional awards, and framed diplomas from medical schools in Siberia, Moscow and Kiev.

'We moved everything to the trauma and maternity wards,' she said. 'They're all we can keep open.'

'Trauma and maternity.'

'It's funny, isn't it? Everyone either fucking or dying.'

'No, not funny.' He stroked his beard, burying his fingers to the first knuckle. His fingers found their way to his beard in moments of trouble or indecision, trawling the thick dark hair but rarely touching upon wisdom. 'They are coming and they are leaving and it is happening here.'

They climbed a stairwell washed in blue emergency light. On the fourth floor she led him down the corridor to the west side of the building. Without warning him she opened the door to the storage room. Something gleeful and malicious shot through her when he took a step back, afraid of falling. 'What happened?' he asked. The floor broke off a metre past the door frame. No walls or windows, just a cityscape muralled across the winter air.

'A few years back we harboured rebels. The Feds blew off the wall in reply.'

'Was anyone hurt?'

'Maali. Deshi's sister.'

'Only one person?'

'A benefit of understaffing.'

On days when both sides abided by the ceasefire, she came to this doorway and looked across the city and tried to identify the buildings by their ruins. The one that flickered with ten thousand pieces of sunlight had been a sheet-glass office building in which nine hundred and eighteen souls had laboured. Beneath that minaret a rotund imam had led the pious in prayer. That was a school, a library, a Young Pioneers' clubhouse, a jail, a grocer's. That was where her mother had warned her never to trust a man who claims to want an intelligent wife; where her father had taught her to ride a bike by imitating the engine growl of a careering municipal bus sure to run her over if she didn't pedal fast enough; where she had solved her first algebra equation for a primary-school teacher, a man for whom Sonja's successes were consolation whenever he pitied himself for not having followed his older brother into the more remunerative profession of prison guard; where she had called for help after witnessing one man spear another on the university green, only to learn they were students rehearsing an Aeschylus play. It looked like a city made of shoeboxes and stamped into the ground by a petulant child. She could spend the whole afternoon rebuilding it, repopulating it, until the hallucination became the more believable reality.

'Before, you couldn't see the river from here,' she said. 'This hospital is the tallest building in the city now.'

There had been tall buildings and plans to erect taller ones. After the dissolution of the USSR, oil reserves had promised prosperity for Chechnya in the coming capitalist century. Yeltsin had told the republics to grab as much sovereignty as they could swallow, and after two thousand years of foreign occupation, it had seemed the republic would finally achieve independence. Her grandparents had moved to Volchansk in 1946 after Stalin added lorry drivers and seamstresses to the expanding list of professions requiring purging, but she felt as buoyantly patriotic as her Chechen classmates who could trace their family trees back to the acorns. That sense of electric optimism was evident in the designs that had been solicited from architects in Riyadh, Melbourne and Minsk. City officials had made a show of the blueprints, displaying them on billboards and distributing them as leaflets at the bazaar. She'd never seen anything like it. The sketches had suggested that the pinnacle of design no longer consisted of cramming the greatest amount of reinforced concrete into the ugliest rectangle possible. Once she had held a leaflet against the horizon and as the red sun bled through the paper the towers had become part of the skyline.

'Did they really want the girl?' she asked, turning her attention back to Akhmed. It didn't surprise her, but she asked anyway. Disappearances touched down as randomly as lightning. Only those actually guilty of abetting the insurgency — an infinitesimal fraction of those abducted — had the benefit of understanding their fate.

'It doesn't make sense,' Akhmed said. Whether he meant the floorless room, the crushed city beyond, or the girl, Sonja didn't know. In the distance, a faint stream of tracers streaked skyward, disappearing into the clouds.

'Payday must be coming,' Akhmed said.

She nodded. The Feds were only paid if they used a certain percentage of their ammo. If the soldiers tired of firing blindly into the sky, they might bury their excess rounds, then dig them up a few hours later to claim the bonus given for discovering a rebel arms cache. 'Let's go,' Sonja said.

They passed the original maternity ward, unused since Maali's death, and descended the stairwell to the new maternity ward. Deshi set down her knitting needles and eyed Akhmed suspiciously as she crossed the room to meet them. After twelve love affairs over the course of her seventy-three years, each beginning with a grander gesture, each ending with a more spectacular heartache, Deshi had learned to distrust men of every size and age, from newborns to great-grandfathers, knowing they all had it in them to break a decent woman's heart. 'Will he be joining us?' she asked.

'Provisionally,' Sonja said.

'And the girl?'

'Provisionally.'

'You're the nurse,' Akhmed said curtly. 'We met earlier.'

'He speaks out of turn, without being addressed,' Deshi observed.

'I just wanted to say hello.'

'He continues to speak without being spoken to. And he has an ugly nose.'

'I'm standing right here,' Akhmed said, frowning.

'He tells us he is standing right here. As if we have been made blind and idiotic.'

'What am I doing wrong?' he asked Sonja. 'I'm just standing here.'

'He seems to believe that his presence might somehow transform the ugliness of his nose, but seeing that nose, right here in front of me, provides irrefutable evidence.'

'What am I supposed to say?' He looked desperately to Sonja. She smiled and turned to Deshi.

'Do you see the way he looks at me?' Deshi asked, her voice trembling with indignation. 'He is trying to seduce me.'

'I'm doing nothing of the sort. I'm just standing here!'

'Denial is the first impulse of a traitor.'

'You're quoting Stalin,' Akhmed said.

'You see? He's a lecher and a Stalinist.'

'Don't be ridiculous.'

'He must be an oncologist.'

'There are few fields of medicine more important than oncology.'

Deshi appeared flabbergasted. 'You see!' she shouted. 'A

lecher, a Stalinist *and* an oncologist? It is too much. It can't be.'

'With respect, I'm thirty-nine and you're old enough to be my mother. I have no desire to have anything but a professional relationship with you.'

'No desire? First he leers, then he insults. Mocking an old woman like me, has he no shame?'

'I'm sorry, OK? I'm sorry. I'm just trying to get along with you.'

Deshi's lips sharpened into a scowl. 'Only a weak man apologises to a woman.'

His eyes were watery by the time Sonja interrupted the exchange. He looked more shocked than he had when she opened the door to the fourth-floor storage room, and through her laughter, she couldn't help feeling guilty for exposing the man to Deshi without warning. 'Enough,' she said. 'Akhmed, this is Deshi. Deshi, Akhmed. Let's work.'

'It's a pleasure,' Deshi said, and returned to the desk beside the incubator.

'What's wrong with her?' Akhmed asked when the nurse was safely out of earshot.

'And now he thinks there's something wrong with Deshi,' Sonja said. A look of horror sank into his face. She assured him she was joking. 'She once fell in love with an oncologist. It didn't work out.'

A woman with dark greasy hair lay in the first bed with a child suckling her left breast. She pulled the bed sheet past the child's head when she saw them approach.

'It's OK,' Sonja said. 'He's a doctor too.'

'But he's a man,' the woman countered.

'This hospital is a madhouse,' Akhmed said, as he turned away. The woman glared at his back, unamused by the implication that her three-day-old son was a lunatic, and then edged the bed sheet down her chest to reveal the child's scrunched face fastened to her nipple.

'The baby is hungry,' Sonja said.

'He'll get used to it,' the woman said, and closed her eyes.

The mother in the next bed slept on her side with her face half swallowed by the pillow. An incubator on a metal cart sat beside her bed. Inside, the infant was underweight and overheated, more like a crushed bird than a human.

'Poor nutrition *in utero*?' Akhmed asked.

'No nutrition *in utero*. Since the second war began, we've only had a handful of mothers healthy enough to give birth to healthy children.'

'And I imagine their fathers aren't civilians?'

'It's not our policy to ask those questions.' She walked to the door. In the corridor she stopped at a darkened light bulb. 'Do you see any moths there?'

'What?'

'Nothing,' she said. In five weeks she would find a moth flapping in the canteen, and wouldn't believe it real until its wings crumpled under her palm. 'The trauma ward is just down the hall.'

Chapter 2

1994 1995 **1996** 1997 1998 1999 2000 2001 2002 2003 2004

WITHIN DAYS AFTER THE PROPOSAL OF THE Khasavyurt Peace Accord, Sonja broke up with her Scottish fiancé, resigned from her post as house officer at the University College Hospital, and sat through connecting flights from London to Warsaw to Moscow to Vladikavkaz. The back seat of the gypsy cab she took from the airport had been removed to allow room for luggage, and her single suitcase slid with the curvature of the road, thudding again and again against the back of her seat, as if to reiterate the lesson that despite the illusions she'd entertained while Brendan's chest rose and receded against hers, her life was small enough to fit inside a piece of luggage. Fuck me, she thought, what am I doing back here?

Dark plumes drifted from distant smokestacks, a chain of wind-rounded mountains, the taste of post-Soviet air like a dirty rag in her mouth. When they reached the bus terminal, she waited until her roller suitcase was safely on the ground before paying the driver. The Samsonite, a final gift from Brendan, might as well have been a neon-lit billboard advertising her foreignness as she rolled it past the imperial-era steamer trunks of other travellers. The nation-alised bus line no longer ran routes into Chechnya, but after she had waited for an hour in a three-person line, a clerk directed her to a kiosk that sold lesbian porn, Ukrainian cigarettes, Air Supply cassettes and tickets on a privately owned bus that made a weekly journey from North Ossetia to Chechnya. The next departure wasn't until the following morning. Though tired from travel, she knew she wouldn't sleep. She sat through the night on a wooden bench with one of her shoelaces tied around the suitcase handle to discourage gypsy children from rolling off with it.

'I am driving you all to your graves,' the bus driver announced as he walked down the aisle to collect tickets at a quarter past six in the morning. He leaned back as though balancing an invisible shot glass on his round stomach. 'If given the opportunity, I will sell you all to the first bandit, kidnapper or slave trader we come across. Don't say you haven't been warned. I wouldn't have to drive *this* bus to *that* country if you hadn't purchased *these* tickets, and for that I will drive over every pothole and divot to make the ride as miserable for you as it will be for me. And no, we will be making no toilet stops, and yes, it is because I know the pain a pothole causes a full bladder.'

She dozed for an hour with her head resting against the window. Every bump in the road was transferred through the glass and recorded by her temple. The sharp pitch of brakes, followed by the bullhorn-amplified instructions of a Russian border guard, brought her back to sudden conscious-ness. The soldiers were all fear and peach fuzz. They ordered the passengers off the bus and demanded each open his or her luggage in a field twenty metres from the road, while they, the waiting soldiers, crouched with their arms wrapped around their legs and their eyes clamped tight, as if jumping into a lake. The poor driver swayed from side to side. Since he was a boy, living on the banks of the Terek, he had dreamed of owning his own tour boat. Six and three-quarter years earlier, just a week before the Berlin Wall fell, the driver had sunk his life's savings into a tour boat, never built, and a contract, never fulfilled, to ferry Party members along the Terek. Now he sat on the ground and rested his back against the tyres of the bus, but the land was a swelling and uncertain ocean and he would feel seasick for many years.

The checkpoint left Sonja charged, and as they crossed from Russian-controlled North Ossetia into Chechnya, she stared through the window she had slept on. On the crater-consumed road the driver made good on his pledge. They passed deserted fields. A toppled farmhouse. A plough resting at the end of a furrow, four months past sowing season. A burning oil well. At the horizon the mountains wore skull-caps of snow. It took ten hours to drive the two hundred kilometres to Volchansk. Checkpoints dotted the highway more regularly than the boarded petrol stations. At each one she carried her suitcase twenty metres from the road and opened it as soldiers held their ears in anticipation.

She spoke to the elderly woman sitting beside her, rolling each word in her mouth like an olive pit before spitting it out, and the woman was a wonderful listener, quiet and attentive as Sonja unfastened the latch to what had been her life until two days prior. She catalogued Brendan's short-comings — his unclipped hangnails, his habit of singing Rodgers and Hammerstein while peeing, his reluctance to correct her grammatical errors — but even as she tried to convince the old woman that Brendan would have made a lousy husband, she missed the way he would write his initials in the pad of her thumb with his hardened hangnails, the way the flush of toilet water accompanied *the hiiiiiiillllls are aliiiiiiiiive with the sound of muuuuuusiiiiic*, the intentional grammatical mistakes he would make, to see if she would catch them, as they took a sledgehammer to the rules of English and reassembled the pieces into a language only they understood. It was wonderful to unburden herself to a sympathetic ear. An hour passed before the old woman pulled a notepad from her purse, scribbled on it and passed it to Sonja. *I thought you would have realised*, the old woman had written. *I'm deaf.*

The four-storey Volchansk terminal was now a one-storey rubble heap. The bus driver held out his hat for tips as they disembarked. 'You will all die in this hellscape,' he cheerfully announced. 'Would you rather your rubles go to your godless murderers, or to me, an honest and pious bus driver, who braves death each week to provide for his family?'

Against her better judgement, Sonja dropped a hyper-inflated thousand-ruble note into the hat, and climbed down before he could curse her. At the next street she caught up with the old woman, who had flagged down a lemon-coloured Lada. The old woman had grown up on a lemon orchard and for her first seventeen years she hadn't eaten a meal that wasn't made of lemon. There had been lemon cucumber salad, lemon vinaigrette beans, lemon-glazed chicken, lemon-stuffed trout, lemon lamb kebab, lemon-dill rice, lemon-roasted chicken thighs, lemon-curd dressing, lemon pudding, lemon-apricot cake, lemon marmalade biscuits, and on it went. She was still four years and one month away from her seventy-sixth birthday and the miracle of her first lime.

The old woman gestured for her to take the cab, and when Sonja refused, she pulled out her notepad and just below *I'm deaf* wrote *Curfew will begin soon and you are younger and prettier than me.*

What had been a delivery van blocked the road three streets from the flat. Sonja climbed out, and the lemon-coloured Lada sped off before she could close the door. The apartment block on the left had lost its exterior wall and she observed the rooms like a mouse peering into a doll's house. She turned to the road where pieces of ground went missing at regular intervals. The land was supposed to be flat, no hills or valleys for fifty kilometres, yet here she was, climbing into a canyon, the dirt wet and thick as she descended asphalt and clay, clambering over broken masonry that had fallen through six storeys of air and one storey of earth, finding her footing on sewage pipes, cursing and kicking the Samsonite when she remembered the instruction booklet's clearly stated direction that the luggage was only suited for paved surfaces, and she was standing at the bottom of the crater when it hit her – *I'm standing at the bottom of a fucking crater!* – and the impact doubled her over, followed immediately by the uppercut of a question – *What am I doing in the bottom of a fucking crater?* – to which the answer was as insubstantial as the word on her lips, three syllables naming the reason for her return – *Natasha* – her sister, haughty, beautiful and unfathomably comfortable in social situations, whom she had last spoken to on the phone the day the first war began, one year, nine months and three weeks earlier, whom she had last seen the day she left for London, four years, eight months and one week earlier, whom she had last envied five years and two months earlier, on the day before the day she received news of the London fellowship, and whom she had last loved at some indeterminate point in the past before they had grown into the people they were to be. She wouldn't climb out of bed for her sister, but she had climbed into a crater. She wouldn't cross a room, but she had crossed a continent.

Her apartment block stood past the bakery where, as a child, she had been given teacakes in exchange for sweeping flour from the floor and repackaging it in brown paper bags. The apartment-block windows were blown out and a line of bullet holes leaked light into the door frame, but it still stood. The front door lay before the threshold like a welcome mat. She climbed to the third floor. Her breaths didn't fill her chest.

Her flat was locked and she knocked on the door and waited, but no pattering footsteps or groaning floorboards answered her. After a fourth quartet of raps led to a fourth silence, she pulled the spare key from her toiletry bag and opened the door. She didn't call out; the thought of her own unheard voice seemed unbelievably sad. Across the room empty window frames held square pieces of twilight. A half-burned candle sat on the dining table, anchored in a shot glass by melted wax. In the past two days she'd slept five hours and an aching exhaustion reverberated through her, tingling her skin. She lit the candle and the small glow fluttered across the egg-white walls. No receipts or envelopes or letters remained, nothing light enough for the wind to carry through the empty frames, nothing on which a goodbye might be written. The furniture was as she remembered: the divan against the right living-room wall, still stained where Natasha had dropped an entire pot of borscht; the black-and-white Ekran television set perched on a milking stool; the wooden kitchen table levelled by three books of matches. This had been her home. This had been her life. That had been her divan. She was returning to it, burying her face in the cushions and weeping into fabric that all these years later still held the scent of beets.

The next morning she went to the doors of the adjacent units. She couldn't recall the names of her neighbours, and judging from her unanswered knocks, they had fled from their flats as from her memory. On the fourth day footsteps came from the hallway. Sonja found a hunched woman wearing a green raincoat even though the sun was shining. The woman carried a dozen plastic shopping bags layered inside each other and tied at the straps.

'Who are you?' the woman asked, with enough suspicion to flatten the question to an accusation. Laina had been on the far side of middle age when Sonja accepted the London fellowship. She had worked the cosmetics counter at the Main Department Store and had gorgeous skin, skin that a thirty-year-old would envy, skin that her supervisor correctly cited as the cosmetic counter's most effective advertisement, skin plied with every moisturiser and emulsion stocked within the glass display case, skin that Sonja and her mother and even her sister had admired, that now looked like the skin of a peach left for many days in the sun.

'I'm Sonja.' Laina's fingertips scrutinised her, holding her wrists, bending her ears. 'I see,' Laina said, at last convinced of Sonja's corporeal form. 'You lived here.'

'I heard you in the hall,' Sonja said a few minutes later, as they drank tea in Laina's flat. 'I thought you were someone else.'

'You shouldn't open the door when you hear strangers. It's never a good idea.'

'It was this once.'

'This is the one in a million.'

'Then I'm very, very lucky.'

'No, you are very, very stupid.'

'Why are you wearing a raincoat? There isn't a cloud for kilometres.'

Laina went to the empty window frames, through which she could see what was left of the city, a view that stretched sixteen blocks further than it had two years earlier. 'I don't trust God. Who knows what He's planning up there.' The bazaar had gradually been repopulated with vendors and sheet-metal kiosks and elderly women like Laina for whom war was no hindrance to a good haggle. She had just bartered a jar of engine oil for sandals that bore the blackened imprints of forty different toes. Once she had had a husband, now dead, whom she could trust not to cheat on her in a brothel. Once she had had a son, now missing, whom she had threatened to marry to Sonja if he misbehaved. Cosmonaut Yuri Gagarin smiled on the face of the clock hanging over the stove, and Sonja studied him as she gathered the breath to dislodge the question that for one and a half years had been wedged in her voice box. When the hour hand fell into the cosmonaut's outstretched palm, she inhaled and asked, 'Do you know where Natasha is?' Laina bit her lip and shook her head. 'I don't know where anyone is.'

No one could answer the question. Days turned to weeks and Sonja accosted the few remaining tenants as they left for work, food, battle or better shelter, but she never received more than a shake of the head, a shrug of the shoulders, an apology. There was no sign of forced entry and the made bed in Natasha's room suggested a deliberate departure. In the bottom chest drawer Sonja found the burgundy cardigan she'd given Natasha for her eighteenth birthday, the one Natasha had hated and called a babushka's jumper, and never wore, not even once, on a chilly day, to appease Sonja. It was just what Natasha would leave behind. She held that sweater, wrapping the arms over her shoulders as if in an embrace.

Hospital No. 6 hired her without requesting an application or CV. When she provided a list of references in London, Deshi crumpled the paper, tossed it under the desk and told

Sonja that Dr Wastebasket would dutifully contact each recommender. Sonja's former professors had fled to the West, to the countryside, to private practices in places where they could save lives without endangering their own. Unimpeded by a hierarchical bureaucracy or institutional memory, she rose from house officer to head surgeon in two months. Landmines didn't obey the Khasavyurt Peace Accord, and within a year she had more trauma surgery experience than the professors she'd studied under. She worked with gratitude for the pain of her patients. In their cries she heard her name as though she were the missing sister, recalled by their gibberish to this place where she amputated limbs and staunched bleeding, where her training was so needed and scarce her patients saw her hovering over the hospital bed as the last prophet of life, whom they pleaded with and praised and spoke to in prayer.

The days were urgent, without pause for reflection beyond the recall of case studies and anatomy lessons. At night she drifted home. If she remembered, she would brush her teeth with baking soda and recite the prayers her mother had taught her. Her tongue fumbled with those awkward and ancient words, and though no one was listening she found a measure of peace in this obsolete language of supplication. After crossing herself, she lay back on the divan and squirted a cool puddle of hand lotion from the bottle she'd brought from London. Invariably she would apply too much, and her hands would be slick and shiny in the candlelight as she asked for another pair with which to share the excess.

The weeks stacked into months that were flipped from the Red Cross calendar hanging behind the waiting-room reception desk; the calendar was from 1993 and would be reused until 2006 and for those thirteen years her birthday would always fall on a Monday. She marked the days, but time didn't march forward; instead it turned from day to night, from hospital to flat, from cries to silence, from claustrophobia to loneliness and back again, like a coin flipping from side to side. Happiness came in moments of unpredictable loveliness. The blind man who played the accordion for her as she splinted the broken leg of his guide dog. The boy who narrated his dreams while recovering from meningitis.

Then, one evening, a knock sounded from the door as she prepared for sleep. She considered and disregarded Laina's advice as the doorknob slipped in her greasy grip. When she opened the door she wanted to scream. Natasha stood right there, in front of her, close enough to hold. She did scream, and she embraced Natasha, and later, on the divan, she took Natasha's hands in her own and rubbed until hers were dry.

Chapter 3

DESPITE AN ADMITTEDLY UNIMPRESSIVE FIRST day, Akhmed left Hospital No. 6 with his eyes on the stars and a swing in his gait. Sure, Sonja was a cold, domineering woman, whose glare could wither flowers and cause miscarriages, and Deshi was clearly a lunatic, and though there wasn't a sliver of compassion between the two of them and the only fate worse than having those two as caretakers was having them as colleagues, it had been a good day. Havaa was safe. His medical training was put to use, and for the first time in months, Ula wasn't his only patient.

He was the first person from Eldár admitted to medical school, an institution so distant and rarefied his inclusion had been celebrated as a village-wide achievement. There had been feasts in his honour, collections to pay for his textbooks. In 1986, Akhmed became the greatest hero in village history since an Eldár barber trimmed the beard of the great Imam Shamil one hundred and forty-one years earlier. There was talk he would move to Volchansk, or even – they would drop their voices to a whisper – Grozny. Anywhere further was too far to dream. Did he realise the hopes the village had pinned on him? Not really. Despite telling Sonja he had graduated from medical school in the top tenth of his class, he had, in fact, graduated in the bottom tenth, the fourth percentile to be precise, and he blamed his inability to find a job on prejudice within the Soviet Medical Bureau rather than on the fact that he had skipped a full year of pathology to attend studio art classes. Eventually the village had offered him an abandoned house on the outskirts, haunted, it was said, by the ghost of a paedophile. He had turned it into a clinic. Even though the villagers overcame their fear of the paedophilic spectre − though many wouldn't let their children enter − and even though their lives were undeniably improved by the presence of a clinic, Akhmed always felt he had let them down, or at least let himself down, by returning to the village that had celebrated his escape. But after applying to twenty-three different hospital positions, and receiving not one interview, he was, today, finally, a physician at Hospital No. 6. And not only a physician, but third in command! When put like that, it was a higher honour than he could have ever imagined. He trekked along the service road more confidently than he had that morning, and imagined what those smug search committees would have had to say about it. They probably wouldn't say anything. They were probably all dead. In this way the war was an equaliser, the first true Chechen meritocracy. He was an incompetent doctor but a decent man, he believed, compensating for his professional limitations with his empathy for the patient, his understanding of pain. Passing the field where the wolf's frozen carcass lay in moonlight, he thought of Marx. Perhaps here was where history had reached its final epoch. A civilisation without class, property, state or law. Perhaps this was the end.

The final fifty metres through the village were the most

dangerous of the eleven-kilometre slog. His footsteps, if over-heard, could prove as lethal as landmines. He slowed as he approached the only house without blackout curtains. The light of generator-powered bulbs burned through the windows. Ramzan, sitting inside, picking at a shiny slice of meat, didn't look like an informer or a collaborator, looked no more menacing than a man in the throes of a mighty indigestion. In the next window, Khassan, Ramzan's father, sat reading at his desk. Khassan hadn't spoken to his son in the two years since Ramzan had begun informing, and though Akhmed never blamed the old man for his son's crimes, the electric bulbs bathed both in the same light.

The glow of their house shrank to a glimmer as he reached his own. The door frame was intact; the door still stood. Opening it, he tensed, waiting for a forceful grip on the shoulder, a rifle butt to the forehead. None came. He lit a kerosene lamp and walked into the bedroom. Ula lay on the bed. She rolled on her side and into the yellow glow.

'Where were you?' she asked. Divorced from tone, the three words still suggested accusation, and he hoped his silence would extinguish her question, as it often did. 'Where were you?' she asked again. Her head barely indented the pillow.

'I went to see Dokka,' he said. 'I helped him shear the sheep.'

She smiled wide enough to show the tips of her teeth. Twelve years earlier those incisors were beloved by the city dentist, a young man who plugged his most lascivious thoughts into the open mouths of young women; but the dentist died a virgin when a misaimed mortar shell landed on his practice and carried him to Paradise in an erupting grey cloud. 'Dokka is so impatient,' she murmured. 'If he waited a month, the flock would give more wool.'

'Yes,' he agreed. 'Dokka was always impatient.' He sat on the bed and set the lantern next to the bedpan and the broth bowl. Each was half full. An ellipsis of wet footprints followed him to the bed. He unlaced his icy boots, massaged the balls of his feet, and lay beside Ula. Once she would have had to roll over to make room for him, but there was less of her now.

'How is his family?'

'They are well,' he said. He turned onto his side and slid his left hand beneath her nightshirt to warm his fingers on her stomach.

'They should eat with us soon,' Ula said.

'They will bring corn and cucumbers,' he whispered to the tiny translucent hairs standing from Ula's earlobe. 'The coals will smoulder on the *mangal* and we will grill *shashlyk* and we will eat in the afternoon and the sun will shine. The lamb is already marinating in Dokka's white plastic bucket with tomatoes and onions and sliced lemons and *uksus*. We will invite Dokka's parents and they will come and perhaps Dokka will bring his chessboard, not the one with the fine wooden pieces, but the plastic one that Havaa gave him for his birthday, the one he said he loved though everyone thought a chess player of his skill would never play on a plastic board. But he did. Do you remember? He taught Havaa to play on it and let her win on her sixth birthday. We will invite them to eat some day.'

'I'm hungry,' she said. 'I don't want to wait that long.'

He pressed his lips to his wife's forehead and let them linger until the kiss became a conversation between their shared skin. How could his wife's sickness both repulse and bind him to her? His love, pity and revulsion each claimed her, each occupied and was driven from her, and even now, as he sealed a postage-stamp-sized square, he was afraid that in moments, when he broke away, his disgust would overwhelm the imprint of his lips.

'I'm hungry,' she repeated. Reluctantly he leaned back. Leaving the lantern beside the bed, he crossed the darkness to the kitchen. After a decade without electricity, his soles knew the way. Eight steps to the living room, a quarter-turn, six to the kitchen threshold, two to the stove. He set firewood on the previous night's ashes, aimed a squirt gun of petrol at the white wood, and struck a match. He prepared a pot of rice and a saucer of powdered milk as the firelight lapped against his legs. While waiting for the rice to cook he pulled a stool to the iron stove and leaned towards the light. He wanted to say something consoling to Dokka, and when his words burned in the stove chamber he hoped the sentiment would rise up the chimney pipe, carried by wind or wing to Dokka's ears, but even if Dokka could hear him, he didn't know what he would say, and he said nothing.

When the rice was moist he scooped it into a ceramic bowl and left the spoon slanting against the rim as he carried the bowl and the mug of powdered milk for two steps, six steps and a quarter-turn in blindness. Was this how a child felt in the womb? He had delivered dozens of newborns, but he couldn't imagine those first few moments. A tear in the shroud and suddenly colours, shapes, coldness, a world of hallucinations.

The lantern cast a circle on the floor and he entered it reluctantly to reach her. He sat beside Ula and brought small spoonfuls of rice to her mouth. Sonja's skill and Deshi's experience didn't matter; neither could care for Ula as he could. 'Was anyone looking for me today?' he asked. She shook her head. 'Are you sure? No knocks at the door? Nothing?'

'I don't think so. I was sleeping.'

'But you would remember if Ramzan called from the door?'

'Oh, yes. Ramzan. He's such a nice man. He always asked my opinion,' she said, and took a sip from the blue mug. 'I think the milk has turned.'

He washed the dishes, undressed and slid beneath the sheets. Her fingers crawled through the covers for his.

'Things are getting worse, aren't they?'

'No,' he said. 'Nothing is getting worse.'

'I don't have much time left, do I?'

These moments were the least bearable, when her meandering trail of questions led to clarity and he couldn't say what was lost to her. Did she really think he'd spent the day shearing sheep sold, slaughtered and consumed long ago? Had she already forgotten Havaa sleeping beside her, the girl's slender body like a splinter of warmth in the dark room, or was the girl the material of dream itself, burned away by morning light? An equally disturbing thought: what if she consciously participated in these delusions to placate him?

'None of us does,' he said, and squeezed her hand.

When her breaths stretched into sleep, he slid his fingers from her loosened grip and contemplated the next day. What would it be like to treat a patient again? Was he capable? Six months had passed since he had last treated patients at the clinic, but he remembered their reluctance as he led them into the examination room, as they realised their bodies had betrayed them once by sickness, and again by forcing them to rely on an incompetent physician. Sometimes he wondered if his own self-loathing manifested itself as harm to his patients, as if some dark part of his heart wanted them to suffer for his failures. And, now, to be confronted with Sonja, a surgeon whose renown had even reached Eldár.

She had asked what he would do with an unresponsive patient, and he, in a blundering moment, had taken it to mean *quiet* or *unwilling to talk*, and had thought of the mute village baker, who communicated only through written notes – which had proved problematic the previous winter when the baker suffered from a bout of impotence he was too ashamed to write down, even to Akhmed. Akhmed had resolved the problem – shrewdly, he thought – by giving the mute baker a questionnaire with a hundred potential symptoms, of which the baker ticked only one, and so had saved the baker's testicles, marriage and pride. But Sonja didn't know that; he'd been too flustered and embarrassed to explain. She had glared at him, knowing that an impostor like him could never belong to the top tenth. She hadn't asked how he had come by her name, why he'd come to her specifically. He hadn't intended to hide the truth from her, but when she didn't ask, he saw no reason to tell her about the chest stitched together with dental floss.

Sonja had made a bedroom of the office of the former geriatrics director, a man she'd never seen but whose tastes conjured an image so defined – browline glasses, a wardrobe predominantly tweedy in character, finely sculpted features, dainty hands – she could have identified his body among the dead. The gerontology department had been closed in the first war due to a scarcity of resources and the general consensus that prolonging the lives of the elderly was a peacetime enterprise. But the director, a bachelor who devoted a healthy portion of his monthly pay cheque to office decor, had the most extravagantly furnished office in the hospital, so of course Sonja was quick to make it hers. A vermilion Tajik rug sprawled across the floor. At the end of the desk stood an antique vase swathed in ornate Persian patterning, beneath which she had found a photograph of a woman framed against the Black Sea, smiling curiously, undated and unidentified, a ghost of the director's life that survived him. Here, the director had spent his life loving a woman he hadn't seen since his twenty-first year, when his father had married her to a Ukrainian for fear of ruinous scandal; the woman was his half-sister, and the love he felt for her caused him so much confusion he could only express it as love for the bewildered and incoherent elderly. The desk was pushed against the wall and on it lay a final payroll still awaiting the director's signature. Six mattresses stacked three abreast formed Sonja's bed, where, after Akhmed had left, she found the girl clothed in limp latex gloves.

'What have you done?' she asked. It was a remarkable sight. The girl had stapled cream-coloured latex gloves to her sweatshirt, to her trousers, had pulled them over her feet, and even wore one on her head like a five-fingered Mohican. 'I repeat, what have you done?'

'See?' the girl asked and stood up. See? See what? She didn't think she needed another reason to renounce children, but here it was: they speak in riddles. 'I see a tremendous waste of medical supplies and I very much wish I wasn't seeing it.'

'See what I am?' the girl asked.

'A nuisance?'

'No, a sea anemone.'

The girl spun in circles. It seemed she was hoping that the gloves would inflate and reach out like tentacles, but those gloves would barely open when Sonja jammed her fingers in them, and they just flailed limply against the girl's chest, back and legs. The whole production seemed so sad that Sonja couldn't muster the anger this profligacy deserved.

'Sea anemones don't talk. Now change into your other clothes.' Sonja nodded to the blue suitcase, still standing beside the mattress where she had left it six hours earlier.

'No. It's my just-in-case suitcase.'

'Just in case what?'

'In case there is an emergency. So I'll have the things that are important to me.'

'There was an emergency,' Sonja said. She sighed. The child was as dense as a block of aged cheese. 'That's why you're here.'

'There might be another one.'

'I'll make a deal with you,' Sonja said, rubbing her eyes. 'Change out of this ridiculous thing and you won't sleep in the car park.'

The girl, who, the previous night, had watched her father's abduction, feared many things, but this bad-tempered and exhausted doctor wasn't among them. She glanced down to the drooping latex gloves; her father would have found her performance enchanting, would have scooped her up in his arms and called her his sea anemone. His approval sparked magic into the blandest day, could layer her in the self-confidence and security she otherwise might lack; and without it, without him, she felt small, and helpless, and the idea of sleeping in a car park suddenly seemed very real. 'I'll change,' she told Sonja with a defeated sag of her shoulders. 'Only if I don't have to unpack.'

'I insist you don't,' Sonja said, turning as the girl undressed. 'It's my greatest wish that you and your suitcase will have vanished into the sea by morning. What's so important in there that you can't unpack?'

'My clothes and souvenirs.'

'Souvenirs? Where have you been?'

'Nowhere.' This was the first night she'd ever spent away

from the village. 'The souvenirs are from people who've stayed at my house.'

When the girl finished changing, Sonja said, 'You have a dirty fingerprint on your cheek. No, not that cheek. The other cheek. No, that's your forehead.' Sonja licked her thumb and rubbed the sooty fingerprint from the girl's cheek. 'Your face is filthy. It's important to stay clean in a hospital.'

'It's not clean to wipe spit on another person's face,' Havaa said defiantly, and Sonja smiled. Perhaps the girl wasn't as dense as she had assumed.

They ate in the canteen at the end of the trauma ward, where Sonja flaunted the hospital's most sophisticated piece of technology, an industrial ice machine that inhaled much of the generator power but provided filtered water. The girl was more impressed by her warped reflection on the back of her spoon. 'It's December. The whole world is an ice machine.'

'Now you're practical,' Sonja said.

The girl made a face at the spoon. 'Can fingers ever grow back?' the girl asked, setting down the spoon.

'No. Why do you ask?'

The girl thought of her father's missing fingers. 'I don't know.'

'How do you know what a sea anemone is, anyway? The nearest sea is a few countries over.'

'My father told me. He's an arborist. He knows everything about trees. I'm still a minimalist.'

'Do you know what that is?'

Havaa nodded, expecting the question. 'It's a nicer way to say you have nothing.'

'Did your father tell you that?'

Again, she nodded, staring down to the spoon head that held her buckled reflection. Her father was as smart as the

47

dictionary sitting on his desk. Every word she knew came from him. They couldn't take what he had taught her, and this made the big, important words he'd had her memorise, recite and define feel for the first time big and important. 'He told me about minimalists and arborists and marine biologists and scientists and social scientists and economists and communists and obstructionists and terrorists and jihadists. I told him about sea anemonists.'

'It sounds like you know a lot of big words.'

'It's important to know big words,' the girl said, repeating her father's maxim. 'No one can take what's inside your head once it's there.'

'You sound like a solipsist.'

'I don't want to learn new words from you.'

Sonja dunked the dishes in a tub of tepid water. Behind her the girl was quiet. 'So your father is an arborist,' she said as she scrubbed their spoons with a grey sponge. It was neither a question nor a statement, but a bridge in the silence. The girl didn't respond.

Back in the geriatrics office she gave the girl a blonde-haired Barbie doll from lost property. It had belonged to the daughter of a devout Warsaw Catholic who believed the makers of department-store toys were conspiring to turn his ten-year-old girl into a heathen, and so he had boxed up all but her Nativity figurines and, filled with the spirit of Christian charity, sent them to a heathen country where they could do no harm to the souls of children already beyond salvation. The doll, dressed in ballroom gown and tiara, appeared surprisingly chipper given her emaciated waistline. The girl inspected the doll, distrustful of this vision of humanity.

'Why is she smiling?' the girl asked.

'She probably found that tiara on the ground and plans to sell it for a plane ticket to London.'

'Or maybe she killed a Russian.'

Sonja laughed. 'Sure, maybe. She could be a *shahidka*.'

'Yes, she's a Black Widow,' the girl said, pleased with the interpretation. 'She snuck into a Moscow theatre and took everyone hostage. That's why she's wearing a dress and jewellery.'

'But where are her hostages? I don't see any. Why else might she be smiling?'

The girl concentrated on the doll's unnaturally white teeth. 'Maybe she's starving and just ate a pastry.'

'What about a biscuit?' Sonja asked, as the idea came to her.

'She'd probably smile if she ate a biscuit.'

'Would you?'

The shadow of the girl's head still bobbed on the wall when Sonja found a chocolate-flavoured energy bar in the upper left desk drawer, a new addition to the humanitarian aid drops, designed for marathon runners. The girl chewed the thick rubber and grimaced. 'What is this?'

'It's a biscuit.'

She shook her head with wide-eyed betrayal. 'This is *not* a biscuit.'

'It's like a biscuit. Biscuit-flavoured.'

'How can something be flavoured like a biscuit and not be a biscuit?'

'Scientists and doctors can make one type of food taste like another.'

'Can you do that?'

If only she could. 'I'm not that type of doctor.'

The girl took another bite, then crinkled the foil around the remnant and slipped it under her pillow.

'It's not that bad,' Sonja said, annoyed by the girl's finicky palate.

'I'm saving it.'

'For what?'

'Just in case.'

The girl lurched against the blankets, but still fell asleep first. Sonja tightened her eyelids and pressed into the pillow but couldn't push herself into oblivion. She only knew how to sleep alone. Since she had returned from London eight years earlier, her casual affairs had never been serious enough to warrant an overnight bag. She sighed. When Deshi woke her that morning, she could have never imagined the day would end like this, with her trying to fall asleep beside this bizarre little thing. Even so, she was glad for Akhmed's help. She needed another set of hands, no matter how fumbling and uncertain they might be. Not that she'd admit it to him. She had to harden him, to teach him that saving a life and nurturing a life are different processes, and that to succeed in the former one must dispense with the pathos of the latter.

The pull of sheets transmitted the girl's shape, her indentation in the mattress, that slight heat burning off her skin. Sonja didn't want her here, couldn't imagine what the girl had seen, or knew, or was blind to or ignorant of that had put her in the Feds' cross hairs. Somewhere a colonel tossed in bed, wanting to find Havaa as much as Sonja wanted her gone, and she would happily trade the girl for Natasha, or her parents, or a plane ticket to London, or a decent night's rest. The girl had lost her father and she had lost her sister and though their shared experience might lead to shared commiseration, she felt cheated. Moths had fluttered on the edge of her vision as she floated into the hallway that after-noon, hoping the man brought news. Her sister had taken the Samsonite when she vanished the previous December. There was no note or explanation, not even under the divan, where Sonja had crawled with a broomstick and the vain hope that the breeze had hidden Natasha's goodbye. It was as if she'd opened the door to the fourth-floor storage closet and fallen off the earth. Poof and gone. But there were no arrest reports, no border-crossing records, no body, and the absence of evidence was enough to allow Sonja to go on hoping that the next patient funnelled through the waiting room, through the swinging doors of the trauma ward would be Natasha. But there had to be a quota. An upper limit to the number of miracles one is privileged to in a lifetime. How many times can a beloved reappear?

The night light coated the girl in a green film. Those smooth, spit-cleaned cheeks gave no indication of the dreams crowding her skull. Should she make it to adulthood, the girl would arrive with two hundred and six bones. Two and a half million sweat glands. Ninety-six thousand kilometres of blood vessels. Forty-six chromosomes. Seven metres of small intestines. Six hundred and six discrete muscles. One hundred billion cerebral neurons. Two kidneys. A liver. A heart. A hundred trillion cells that died and were replaced, again and again. But no matter how many ways she dismembered and quantified the body lying beside her, she couldn't say how many years the girl would wait before she married, if at all, or how many children she would have, if any; and between the creation of this body and its end lay the mystery the girl would spend her life solving. For now, she slept.

Chapter 4

1994 1995 1996 1997 1998 1999 2000 2001 2002 2003 **2004**

A SHADOW APPEARED AGAINST THE WHITE horizon, filling the sleeves of a familiar navy overcoat. Two mornings earlier, Akhmed would have waved and walked to greet his friend. He would have walked until the shade dissolved from Khassan's face and then walked further, to raise his voice, without fear or hesitation, had this been two mornings earlier. But these were afterthoughts as he ran into the forest and hid behind a grey trunk only half his width. He crouched at the base of the trunk and gulped the dawn air and hoped Khassan, a sharpshooter in the Great Patriotic War, hadn't seen him flee. He cradled his jaw in his palms. Was this how he would live now? Fleeing into the forest at the slightest rustle?

Three taps sounded on the birch trunk. 'Is anyone home?' the old man asked. Akhmed stood and turned ruefully. His footprints led right to the tree trunk. From the wrong ends of binoculars, Khassan could have tracked him here.

'It's cold to be out so early,' Akhmed said. He couldn't raise his gaze above Khassan's shoulders as they walked back to the service road. The old man's frame still filled his overcoat and he held a two-kilogram weight in each hand. At the age of seventy-nine – a full twenty years past the life expectancy of the average Russian man, as he often pointed out – Khassan maintained the exercise regimen he had begun in the army a half-century earlier. Fifty squats, sit-ups and press-ups, plus a five-kilometre run that had slowed to a saunter over the decades.

'My balls have frozen in Poland and in Nazi Germany and in Kazakhstan. They have frozen in nine different time zones. But now?' He sighed and gazed sorrowfully at his crotch. 'Now I'm too old to need them, so why should I care if they freeze?'

As a child and an adult, Akhmed had been captivated by stories of Khassan's sixteen-year odyssey. To a man who had never even been to Grozny, Khassan's travels rose to the realm of legend. In 1941, the Red Army gave him five bullets and an order to find a gun among the dead. With a rifle prised from frozen fingers in Stalingrad, he shot a path through Ukraine, Poland and Germany. He pulled two bullets from his left thigh, lost three friends to hypothermia, killed twenty-seven Nazis by bullet, four by knife, three by hand, fought under five generals, liberated two concentration camps, heard the voices of innumerable angels in the ringing of an exploded mortar, and took a shit in one Reichstag commode, a moment that would for ever commemorate the war's victorious conclusion. After his years of service he returned to a Chechnya without Chechens. While he had fought and killed and shat for the USSR, the entire Chechen population had been deported to Kazakhstan and Siberia under Stalin's accusations of ethnic collaboration with the fascist enemy. His commanding officer, a man whose life Khassan had twice saved, was to spend the next thirty-eight years working as a train porter in Liski, where the sight of train rails skewering the sun to the horizon served as a daily reminder of the disgraceful morning he shipped Khassan, the single greatest soldier he'd ever had the pleasure of spitting orders at, to Kazakhstan on a train packed with Russian physicians, German POWs, Polish Home Army soldiers and Jews. Khassan's parents hadn't survived the resettlement, and in 1956, when – after the death of Stalin three years earlier – Khrushchev allowed Chechen repatriation, Khassan disinterred their remains and carried them home in their brown suitcase.

'From what you told me,' Akhmed said, 'they weren't cold from disuse.'

Khassan smiled. 'Thank goodness the borders are closed. Who knows how many Fräuleins might otherwise track me down for dowries?'

Violet light veined the clouds. Akhmed searched for something to say, a sentence flung to pull them from the sinkhole of Dokka's disappearance. 'How's the book?'

Khassan winced. Not the right sentence. 'I'm giving up on that,' he said.

'It's not writing itself?'

'History writes itself. It doesn't need my assistance.'

'But it's your life's work.'

'Your life's work could be scrubbing piss from a toilet bowl. Work isn't meaningful just because you spend your life doing it.'

For four decades Khassan had drafted and redrafted his six-volume, 3,300-page historical survey of the Chechen lands. Akhmed was a child when he had first seen the pages. After cancer had put his mother in the ground, he and his father had received weekly invitations to dine with Khassan in the three-room house built by Khassan's father in a time when men were expected to grow their own corn, raise their own sheep and build their own homes. A partial draft, kept in eight boxes beneath Khassan's desk, was written in the careful cursive of a condolence letter. Akhmed found it one afternoon while his father and Khassan sat outside, gossiping like married ladies beneath a June sun. Each afternoon, while Khassan taught at the city university, Akhmed snuck into the living room and stole a single page. He read it at night, after completing his homework, and exchanged it the next afternoon for the following page. Khassan had begun his history in the time before humanity, when the flora and fauna of Chechnya had existed in classless egalitarianism. In a twenty-page account of Caucasian geology, Khassan proved that rock and soil adhered to the same patterns of dialectical materialism proffered by Marx. A seven-page explanation of natural selection compared kulaks to a species that failed to adapt to environmental changes. Akhmed read seventy-three pages in total, only reaching the Neolithic period before Khassan realised pages had gone missing: the three Akhmed had lost, the two he had turned into paper aeroplanes, and the one, a description of Eldár Forest before man invented chainsaws, that had been too beautiful for him to return. Believing the culprit to be a secret police informant, Khassan had burned the pages in his wood stove.

'But you need to finish it,' Akhmed urged, unsure if Khassan was serious. The Khassan obsessed with a history book that, even if published, no one would read was the only Khassan he knew. Khassan could renounce his legs and sound no more ridiculous.

'You're right,' Khassan said. His parted lips revealed a row of teeth the colour of cooking oil. That city dentist had been so in love with the teeth of his young women patients, he couldn't look inside the mouth of an old man for more than a few moments without feeling a wash of revulsion and betrayal; he had never told Khassan to floss. 'And I'm sorry, Akhmed. For Dokka.'

'Was he taken to the Landfill?'

Khassan's shoulders sloped in a shrug. They both knew the answer but that didn't make it any easier to admit. 'I don't know. I don't know anything.'

'Can you ask Ramzan . . .' Ask him what? Ramzan had no answers; the blindness he walked through was a shade darker than theirs. 'Can you ask him to let the girl be? She's gone.'

'Ramzan hasn't heard my voice in the one year, eleven months and three days since he began informing. I've counted every day of silence. It's stupid, I know, but silence is the only authority I have left.'

Each looked past the other, into the woods stretching on either side of the road, uncomfortable and ashamed. 'I'm a pariah. The father of an informer,' Khassan continued. 'You and my son are the only people in the village willing to speak to me, and I can't speak to him. In one year, eleven months and three days the only conversations I've had have been with you. You still speak to me. Why?'

Akhmed focused on the trees. He didn't know. He didn't know that when Khassan returned home that morning he would write down what he remembered of their conversation in a shorthand his son couldn't decipher, or that later Khassan would read it quietly, without speaking a single word aloud, and even on the page their exchange would lift that blanketing silence like tent poles. What he did know was that Khassan was his friend, a decent man, and that was as rare as snowfall in May.

'You ran away from me just now,' Khassan said, before Akhmed could answer. 'I understand. My son is weak and cruel. That's fine. You know, I've been thinking of the

Festival of the Sacrifice recently. In the resettlement camps we celebrated in secret, slaughtering a wild dog in place of a lamb. I wonder if Ibrahim's palms were damp as he walked his son to the summit. Did he tell him they were going on a hike? Did he take water? I think he must have glared at the knife until his reflection was part of the blade. I think relief must have replaced his horror when he unsheathed his knife and recognised his face. He must have known that what he was to do was of such significance it had already become who he was, and so he offered both his son and himself to the *kinzhal*'s edge.'

Hunched over, Khassan pressed his bare hands into the snow. He sank them to his forearms and left them there in what a stranger might take to be a demonstration of endurance, but what was, Akhmed knew, a private ritual of contrition. His face was broken in a way Akhmed couldn't look at, let alone understand, let alone mend. 'Walk on both sides of the service road so my footprints can't be followed,' Akhmed said. 'I'll be gone all day. Make sure no one knows where I'm going. Do that.'

Khassan's head bobbed. He scooped two palmfuls of snow and pressed them to his eyes. Melting rivulets circled his wrists. 'Ibrahim's willingness to sacrifice his son isn't hard to believe. His son was an innocent. It's so much harder when you know what your son would do to you if he survived. When you know just what would happen if an angel was to grab the knife from your hand.'

Distal phalange, proximal phalange, metatarsus, medial cuneiform, navicular, talus, calcaneus. Akhmed recited the bones composing the big toe and followed the Latin north to the ankle as he walked to the hospital. Before leaving that morning he had torn a half-dozen diagrams from his old anatomy textbook and he studied them as he hiked, glancing up every few seconds to check for landmines. He'd be ready for any more of Sonja's quizzes. The sun had fully risen when he entered the hospital and the guard, whose left arm ended at the elbow, stopped him.

'Here?' he asked, exasperated. 'I've walked nearly to Turkey avoiding checkpoints.'

The cuff of the guard's left jacket sleeve was sewn to his shoulder. The slender beard descending from his chin looked like the tail of a squirrel hibernating in his mouth. 'You need to pull the glass shards from your boots,' the guard instructed.

'Don't worry,' Akhmed said. 'I'm the doctor.'

'No, Sonja is the doctor,' the one-armed guard corrected. 'You are the idiot with glass shards in his boot soles. Now have a seat on that bench and take those pliers and pull out the glass if you want to enter the hospital.'

No one could walk through the city without lodging a full pane of glass shards in his shoe soles, and the guard, who had for eighteen arduous months fought with the rebels and had witnessed and participated in all manner of horrors, was afraid of Sonja and what she would do if she found glass shards tracked into the hospital. He watched Akhmed prise out fourteen shards and deposit them in an ashtray.

Akhmed sighed, crestfallen. His first day as a hospital doctor wasn't beginning well. 'Tell me,' he asked, nodding to the guard's missing arm, 'do they pay you half rate?'

The guard, thirty-one years old, had never received a pay cheque, and wouldn't have known what to do with one if he had; in three years, when the hospital issued pay cheques again, beginning with a whopping nine years of back pay, the guard would frame his in glass and hang it on his wall without ever depositing it. For the rest of his life, he wouldn't trust the numbers people put on paper. 'They should pay me more than they pay you,' the guard said, smiling. 'Even I know better than to give an unresponsive patient a questionnaire.'

Akhmed's flush hadn't faded when he pushed open the double doors. The cannonball of Havaa's head crashed into his stomach.

'You came back!' she exclaimed, breathless from her sprint across the room. He raked his fingers through her almond-brown hair, a shade shared by the back of his hand. He had been so concerned with Latin nomenclature he'd forgotten about her, and as her arms formed a tourniquet around his waist, the tight press slowed his breaths. She hadn't forgotten him for a moment.

'Of course I came back. Where else would I go?'

'Has he——' she began, and he squeezed her shoulder as consolingly as he was able.

'We'll both be here a little longer, OK?'

'I guess,' she said. She loosened her embrace and stepped back as the enthusiasm of the prior moment drained from her face. Her blue suitcase stood by the folding chair where she had been sitting.

'Planning on going somewhere?'

'In case we were going home,' she said. Again Akhmed squeezed her shoulder, but the gesture was small and futile, and reasserted the helplessness she seemed to foist upon him.

'How was your night?' he asked, hoping to cheer her up. 'Did Sonja turn into a bat after the sun went down?'

She shook her head.

'Are you sure?'

'Yes,' Havaa said, dropping her voice to a whisper. 'She just became boring. She wouldn't stop talking about her ice machine. And she called me a solipsist.'

Akhmed followed her across the waiting room to the perimetre of paint-chipped folding chairs and sat down beside her. She lifted the blue suitcase to her lap and wrapped her arms around it. 'Do you want me to carry that back to your room?' he offered. She gave a slow, dejected shake of her head, raised the suitcase on its side and hugged it. 'You know what you should do,' he said, turning to her. 'You should teach the guard downstairs to juggle.'

'But he only has one arm.'

'But he really wants to learn. He's embarrassed by his arm so he'll refuse at first. But you need to be persistent.'

'I can be persistent,' she said.

'Yeah?'

'My father says persistence is a polite way of being annoying.'

'You're good at that, aren't you?'

With a slight smile, she acknowledged her considerable expertise. But the smile he had worked for wilted when the trauma doors swung open and Sonja walked in. Each step produced a rattle from her bleached-white scrubs. Pink veins cobwebbed her eyes. 'You're late,' Sonja snapped, completely oblivious to the important work happening there, on the waiting-room chairs, between them.

He raised his eyebrows to Havaa and then followed Sonja into a corridor cloaked in curtains of pungent ammonia. She turned into the staff canteen, where, in the corner, the notorious ice machine brooded. Sheets and towels draped from clothes lines and silver instruments shifted in pots of boiling water. Gaffer tape covered the windowpanes and the overhead emergency lights cast a dull blue glow across the walls. Even in war conditions he had expected Hospital No. 6 to be more glamorous than this.

'Was everything all right with Havaa last night?' he asked.

Sonja didn't turn to him. 'Let's say she's an inexperienced house guest,' she said, and felt the hanging sheets for moisture. She handed him scrub tops from the furthest clothes line. Still damp.

'What about the ones I wore yesterday?' he asked. 'I left them in a cupboard down the corridor.'

'No, they need to be clean. And just as important, they need to be white.'

'Why white?'

She leaned against the wall and slid her hands into the cavernous pockets of her scrub bottoms. He concentrated on her face as if preparing to draw her portrait – the angles, ratios and proportions of her features – all so he wouldn't have to meet her eyes.

'Our appearance is as important as anything we do. Our patients need to believe we operate no differently from a hospital in Omsk,' she said, and, elbow-deep, pulled a cigarette from her pocket.

'So the perception of professionalism is more important than being professional?' It was an idea he could stand behind.

She raised her chin and blew a line of smoke at the ceiling. 'We're three people running a hospital that requires a staff of five hundred. We need to appear to be consummate professionals because it's the only way we'll fool anyone into thinking we are.'

'So, right now, because you're smoking a cigarette and I'm not, I'm the more professional of us two?'

Her laughter rang more pleasantly now that it wasn't at his expense, and he watched with satisfaction as she dipped the ember into a puddle collecting beneath the clothes line, and flicked the butt into the wastebasket. 'You're walking two steps ahead of your shadow.'

'About that, I was thinking that since this is my first day, it might be better if I didn't begin working one-on-one with patients immediately.'

'That might be the best idea you've ever had,' she said, and handed him the rest of the scrubs. When he began to undress, she took her time looking away.

Patients funnelled into the trauma ward – a young man with a deep tubercular cough, an elderly woman whose hair had caught on fire, two teenagers who had beaten away half their faces as they negotiated the ownership of a supposedly lucky rooster's claw – and Akhmed, thankful, attended to none of them. It might feel good to be back between the earpieces of a stethoscope, but it felt much better to be in the canteen, where no calamity greater than a cross word from Deshi befell him. He spent the morning following her, nodding politely as she denounced the Russians for various earthly ills, and a few – volcanoes, winter, her arthritic hips – that fell within God's jurisdiction.

'If we could, we'd blame constipation on the Russians,' he said.

'I already do. Roughage is so rare.' She picked a pair of brown trousers from the pile on the floor and emptied its pockets on the worktop. A scatter of folded paper, loose change, keys, plastic cards and lint fell out. She slid all but the identity card and loose change into the bin.

'Anything good in this one?' he asked. It was the four-teenth pair of trousers Deshi had laid on the worktop that morning, the fourteenth she had searched for money, cigar-ettes, whatever else the dead man hadn't thought to use before he went on his way. 'Maybe a plane ticket?'

'A plane ticket.' She waved her hand to dismiss the very breath that carried so stupid a question. 'Where would he go, anyway?'

'I don't know. Grozny.'

'Grozny?' She gaped at him. Every Saturday from 1976 to 1978 Deshi had met the seventh of her twelve great loves, an oil geologist, in the suite of the Grozny Intourist Hotel, until the Saturday night she walked in to find him occupied with another nurse; she would never forgive the city for harbouring that man. 'Is he serious?'

'I've never been to Grozny,' Akhmed said.

'If he could go anywhere, he'd choose Grozny?'

'I've never been there before,' he said softly. In the decade and a half since he'd left medical school, he'd forgotten just how wide the world stretched beyond his village, just how provincial and unremarkable his little life was when compared with nearly anything. Deshi, who, judging from her tone of disapproval, would be impressed with nothing short of a circumnavigation of the globe, was quick to remind him.

'Unbelievable,' she sighed, and turned her back to him. She glanced at the identity card to see if the trousers belonged to an acquaintance, then tossed it into a shoebox filled with several dozen others. It was a simple gesture, no more than a flick of her fingers, performed without malice or contempt, but with complete uninterest, and it cut through Akhmed like a fin through water. In her indifference he saw the truth of a world he didn't want to believe in, one in which a human being could be discarded as easily as pocket lint. But Deshi was no longer paying attention to him. 'Grozny,' she muttered. 'Small-minded and an idiot doctor. He'd probably prescribe *kalina* berries for pneumonia. And that gargoyle squatting where his nose should be. Long enough to keep the tips of his toes dry in a rain shower.'

She turned the trouser legs inside out and spread them on the worktop; a pouch protruded from the inside leg, just below the knee, where it was sewn in with black thread. She ran a razor blade across the stitching, and removed a few crumpled notes and a folded sheet of paper. Akhmed's stomach clenched as she reached towards the waste bin with the sheet of paper. 'Wait,' he said. He knew what was written on it, knew the time had passed to provide for any final request, but asked anyway. 'What does the note say?'

Deshi frowned. ' "*90 October the 25th Road, Shali*," ' she read. ' "*Return me for burial.*" Too late, my friend. You should have stitched your note to the outside of your trousers.'

'Where is the body?'

'Already in the clouds. It's sacrilege, I know, but they burn nearly every body that isn't claimed. Can't come by a body bag these days. The Feds requisition them to make field *banyas* while on patrol. The strangest thing I've ever seen, three hundred soldiers, naked as the day they were born, huddled within black plastic bags that trapped the steam of cold water poured over stone fires. Only a Russian could find pleasure inside a body bag.'

As she refolded the note and dropped it into the waste bin, he wanted to reach out, to snatch the tumbling rectangle before it landed and was lost among the last words of two dozen others who died far from their villages, who were pitched by strangers into furnaces, who were buried in cloud cover and wouldn't return home until the next snowfall. Akhmed's own address was written on a slip of folded paper and stitched into his left trouser leg, where with every step it chafed against his leg, awaiting the decent soul that would one day carry him, should he die away from home.

'What's his name?' he asked. That man had a sister in Shali who would have given her travel agency — now no more than a once-prestigious name — her parents-in-law and nine-tenths of her immortal soul to hold that note now lying at the bottom of the waste bin, if only to hold the final wish of the brother she regretted giving so little for in life.

In the shoebox the identity cards were layered eight-deep. She held a card to the light and set it back down. 'He's one of these,' she said.

While Sonja spent her afternoon in surgery, Akhmed spent his in the canteen, folding bed sheets into rectangles that soon filled the wicker laundry baskets. At first he had protested, complaining it was the duty of a maid, until Sonja reminded him that those were the only duties he was qualified to perform. While folding he imagined his wife lying on a greyer bed sheet, her head propped on her favourite of their two pillows, the thick foam one that cramped his neck on those nights when they fell asleep sharing it. If she had the energy, she might lift one of his art books from the stack beside the bed. Those hard clothbound covers held worlds of marble statues, woodblock prints, lily pads, bouquets, long-dead generals, and placid landscapes where aristocrats in funny hats pranced around. At night he narrated the scenes to her as if he knew what he was talking about, inventing biographies for every portrait, intrigues for each glance within a frame. Since he had first started skipping first-year pathology to attend still-life drawing classes, he had maintained an abiding interest in art, and for a man who had never been to Grozny, he had amassed a respectable collection of art books. Each morning he reordered the stack so that the first book she reached for was new to her.

He folded the sheet and set it beside the others. How long since he'd last changed Ula's sheets? Ten days, at least. She rarely rolled from her side of the bed, and when he carried her to the living-room divan and stripped the linen from the mattress, he found her tawny silhouette sweated into the fabric. That musky darkening was so particularly, irrevocably Ula that he would hesitate to wash it. But then, scolding himself for being sentimental, he would fill the basin with soapy water and submerge her outline and watch her disappear. He was losing her incrementally. It might be a few stray brown hairs listless on the pillow, or the crescents of bitten fingernails tossed behind the headboard, or a dark shape dissolving in soap. As a web is no more than holes woven together, they were bonded by what was no longer there. The dishes no longer prepared or eaten, no more than the four- and five-ingredient recipe cards stacked above the stove. The walks no longer walked, the summer woods, the undergrowth unparted by their shins. The arguments no longer argued; no stakes, nothing either wanted or could lose. The love no longer made, desired, imagined or mourned. The illness had restored to Ula an innocence he was unwilling to pollute, and the warmth of her flesh cocooning his was a shard of their life dislodged from both their memories.

It had begun in late spring 2002, a year after the *zachistka* that claimed the lives of forty-one villagers, on the morning she slept through breakfast. 'I feel sick,' she mumbled, and he carried her tea to the bedside table. Had he known the cup was the first of hundreds he would take to her bedside, he would have made a more bitter brew. He took her temperature, pulse and blood pressure: all normal. Her eyes were clear, her skin coloured. When asked she couldn't provide a coherent description of her pain. It was like a loose marble tumbling around her insides, migrating from her ankle to her knee to her hip, and back down. Some days her toes contained all her hurt. Or her fingers. Or elbows. Or kidneys. Eventually it settled somewhere between her chest and stomach, only leaking into her legs on Mondays. Pain is symptomatic rather than causal, even he knew that, and the only reasonable conclusion was that the sickness was seated in her mind. But while he didn't believe she was physically sick, he couldn't deny the reality of her suffering. A year earlier the *zachistka* had levelled a third of the village. Angels descended. Prophets spoke. Truth was only one among many hallucinations.

For the first few weeks he had resisted taking her to Hospital No. 6. He may have graduated in the bottom tenth of his class, but he was still a licensed doctor, and a decent one, even if he didn't always know what he was doing. What would people say if they knew he couldn't diagnose his own wife? Already his patients rarely paid their bills; if news of his ineptitude spread, they would starve. But a month passed without decline or recovery and this static state, this purgatorial non-progression, finally convinced him that his wife's illness exceeded his abilities. He tried to take her to the hospital. Three times they ventured to Volchansk in Ramzan's red pickup, but army cordons blocked all roads into the city. He dreamed up and in his notebook drew ways of conveying her: a sedan chair, a tunnel, a kite large enough to lift her bed. After the fourth attempt, when an unspooled shell casing popped Ramzan's tyre ten metres past the house, he gave up. What would the hospital doctors say anyway? With so many real injuries to tend to, they would dismiss Ula and her phantom sickness. The thought of her forced to defend her pain made his fingers curl into fists.

For eight and a half months he cared for her with paternal devotion. But each morning as he set the teacup on the bedside table, he wondered if physical deprivation might revive her ailing mind, and so, ten days before Dokka lost his fingers, Akhmed left her teacup in the kitchen. As the day wore on she called his name in cries more confused and desperate with each iteration, until his name was no longer his but a word of absolute anguish. Unable to stand the call of his name, he stayed with Dokka's wife and daughter for three nights. On the fourth morning he returned and found her on the bedroom floor. The beginnings of bedsores reddened her shoulder blades. In that moment he came to understand that he would spend the rest of his life atoning for the past three days, and that the rest of his life wouldn't be long enough. He lifted her from the floor and set her beneath the sheets. He took her a glass of water from the kitchen, then five more. 'You never have to get up again,' he promised her. He laid his head on her chest and her heart pattered against his temple. 'Akhmed,' she said. 'Akhmed.' His name was now a lullaby.

He never again tried to coerce Ula into health. It would end. Everything did. But when he emptied the bedpan in the backyard, or brushed her teeth despite her protestations, the afterglow of resentment still smouldered. She was gone but still there, the phantom of the wife the war had amputated from him, and unable to properly mourn or love her, he cared for and begrudged her. And so the previous day, when he had offered to work at the hospital until other accommodations could be found for Havaa, he had hoped Sonja would agree for his sake as much as the girl's. That morning, when he left Ula alone with four glasses of water and a bowl of lukewarm rice on the bedside table, he double-locked the door and entered the dawn chill with the confidence that Havaa's future meant more than his wife's, and he trudged eleven kilometres through a broken obligation that only a child's life could justify.

When he folded the last sheet he ducked beneath the clothes lines and opened the cupboard. His trousers lay folded on the bottom shelf. Along the left inside leg he found a familiar bulge in the stitching. If he were to die away from home, he hoped a kinder soul than Deshi would find him.

'Tomorrow we'll go to Grozny,' Sonja announced as she strode through the canteen doorway, stopping at the worktop to inspect the scalpels he'd boiled.

'Did Deshi tell you that?' he asked, unable to mask the panic building behind his eyes. 'I was only kidding. Of course I'd use the plane ticket to go somewhere else. Tbilisi, even Istanbul.'

'You boiled these for ten minutes?'

'You're joking, right?'

She gestured towards him with the scalpel blade, a little too casually for Akhmed's comfort. 'About ten minutes in boiling water? I've never been more serious.'

'No, about Grozny.'

'Did you or did you not boil these for ten minutes?'

'Yes, but are we going to Grozny?'

She frowned, seeming to think *he* was the one talking in circles. 'You don't get to ask any more questions,' she said. 'A question mark in your mouth is a dangerous weapon.'

'So are we?'

She gave a defeated sigh. 'Yes.'

'Why?'

She pulled a cigarette lighter from her pocket. 'Do you smoke?'

'I am an excellent cigarette smoker.' It had been seven weeks since his most recent cigarette, and two months more since the one before that, and technically those had been *papirosi*, capped with a filterless cardboard tube and jammed with coarse tobacco that left him violently nauseous for the rest of the day.

Perhaps inspired by his earlier display of professionalism, she waited until they reached the car park before lighting up. She passed him the square pack. He knew the Latin alphabet, but hadn't used it in years. 'Duh . . .'

'Dunhill,' she said.

He selected one from the two erect rows and leaned it into Sonja's lighter. The first drag slid into his lungs without the paint-scraper harshness of his two most recent cigarettes, and he stared at the slowly burning ember, admiring the quality of the tobacco and the quality of the flame, pleasantly surprised that he didn't feel ill. 'Where did you get these?' he asked.

'Grozny.'

'We're going there to get cigarettes?'

She smiled. 'I can't believe you'd really use that plane ticket to go there.'

'I've never been.'

'It's something else.'

'So why are we going?'

Further down the street the side of a building had crushed all the vehicles in a car park. He was thirty-nine years old and had hoped to own a car by this age.

'I go once a month to pick up supplies,' Sonja said. 'Not just cigarettes. About everything in the hospital comes through a man I know in Grozny with connections to the outside. I also call a friend of mine who lives in London and updates me on what's been going on in the world.'

'What's happening out there?' he asked. By now the wider world was no more than a rumour, a mirage beginning at the borders. Thirty-two years earlier, in the rancid air of his primary school — built on a street bookended by a sewage treatment facility and a lumberjack brothel — his geography teacher had expected him to believe that the world was the same shape as a football. He had been the first of his class-mates to accept it, not because he knew anything about gravity, but because the air was more nauseating than usual that afternoon, and he wanted to leave. For the rest of her career that geography teacher would pride herself on being the first to recognise Akhmed's aptitude for the sciences.

'Last month he told me that George Bush had been re-elected,' Sonja said.

'Who's that?'

'The American president,' Sonja said, looking away.

'I thought Ronald McDonald was president.'

'You can't be serious.' There it was again, condescension thick enough to spread with a butter knife. His mother was the only other woman to have spoken to him like that, and only when he was a child – and only when he wouldn't eat his cucumbers.

'Wasn't it Ronald McDonald who told Gorbachev to tear down the wall?'

'You're thinking of Ronald Reagan.'

'English names all sound the same.'

'That was fifteen years ago.'

'So? Brezhnev was General Secretary for eighteen.'

'It doesn't work like that over there,' she explained. 'They have elections every few years. If the president doesn't win, someone else becomes president.'

'That's ridiculous.' The wind lifted the ash from his cigarette and scattered it across the empty car park.

'And you can only be president for ten years,' she added.

'And then what? You become prime minister for a bit and then run for president again?'

'I think you just step down.'

'You mean Ronald just stepped down after ten years?' he asked. She had to be putting him on.

'He just stepped down and George Bush became president.'

'And then George Bush shot Ronald Reagan to prevent him seizing power?'

'No,' she said. 'I think they were friends.'

'Friends?' he asked. 'It makes me wonder how we lost the Cold War.'

'Good point.'

'And so George Bush has been president since Ronald Reagan?'

'There was another guy in there. Clinton.'

'The philanderer. I remember him,' he said, pleased. 'And then George Bush became president again?'

'No, the George Bush who is president now is the first George Bush's son.'

'Ah, so that's why they don't shoot the previous president. They're all related. Like the Romanovs.'

'Something like that,' she said distractedly.

'Then who is Ronald McDonald?'

'You know, Akhmed,' she said, looking at him for the first time in several minutes, 'I'm beginning to like you.'

'I'm not an idiot.'

'You used the word, not me.'

A blast rippled from the east, a long wave breaking across the sky.

'A landmine,' she said, as if it were no more than a cough. 'We should get going.'

He dropped his cigarette without finishing it, the first time he'd done so in six years, and was careful to avoid the glass shards as he followed her back to the entrance.

'Sew the pockets of your trousers before you come in tomorrow,' she advised. 'We'll pass a dozen checkpoints to reach Grozny and with that beard you look like a fundamentalist. I don't want the soldiers to plant anything on you.'

Akhmed looked to the clouds before following her into the corridor. It wouldn't matter even if he had found a plane ticket. Ten and a half years had passed since he had last seen commercial aircraft in the sky.

The man dragged into the waiting room wasn't the first landmine victim Akhmed had ever seen, not the first he'd seen accompanied by an incomprehensible woman, not even the first he'd seen dragged on a tarpaulin along a slick scarlet trail; he wasn't the first man Akhmed had seen writhing like a lone noodle in a pot of boiling water, not the first he'd seen with half his shin hanging by a hinge of sinew. But when Akhmed saw this man it was like seeing the first man for the first time: he couldn't think, couldn't act, could only stand in shock as the air where the man's leg should have been filled the floor and the room and his open mouth. The woman tugging at the corner of the tarpaulin spoke a language of shouts and gasps and looked at him as if he could possibly understand her. What a volume her chest produced. The true colour of her dress was indistinguishable for the blood. When he finally remembered how to use his feet, he walked right past the woman and the writhing man, to the corner chair, where he draped a white lab coat over Havaa's head.

Then the man's pulse was a haphazard exertion against his finger. The woman was asking one question after the next. Her dress was showing the curves of her legs. Her breath was on his left cheek. An artery was severed. His face was pale yellow. Sonja was there. She was strapping a rubber tourniquet below the knee. She was rolling him on a gurney and into the hall. The gurney was turning into the operating theatre and Deshi was taking the man's blood pressure. 'Sixty over forty,' she was calling out. The blood-pressure metre was Velcroed to the young man's arm. The bulb was swinging above the gurney wheel. The wound was wet with saline.

With swift, well-rehearsed movements, Sonja inserted IVs of glucose and polyglukin into the man's arms. She pulled a surgical saw from the cabinet and disinfected the blade as Deshi called out blood-pressure readings. At seventy over fifty, she injected lignocaine just above the tourniquet. Deshi anticipated her requests, and the clamps he'd boiled were in her reach before she asked. She worked without looking at the man's face or hearing his cries as though her patient were no more than his most grievous wound. Blood reached her elbows but her scrubs remained white. The man, and he was a man, it was so easy to forget that with all his insides leaking out, had graduated from architecture school and had been searching for employment when the first bombs fell. When the landmine took his leg, he had already spent nine years searching for his first architectural commission. Another six and three-quarter years would pass before he got that first commission, at the age of thirty-eight. With only twenty per cent of the city still standing, he would never be without work again.

'Come here,' Sonja called. Akhmed looked over his shoulder to summon a more capable ghost from the Brezhnev-beige wall. 'Akhmed, come here,' she repeated. He stepped forward, wiggling his toes in his boots. One step and then the next, with an immense gratitude for each. The skin was peeled back towards the knee. The calf muscle cut away. The bone wasn't wider than a chair leg.

She gestured with her scalpel. 'For a below-the-knee amputation, you want to keep in mind that stumps close to the knee joint will be difficult to fit for a prosthesis. Long stumps are also difficult to fit and can lead to circulation issues. First, you'll need to make a fish-mouth incision superior to the point of amputation. You want a posterior flap long enough to cover the padded stump and to ensure a tensionless closure when sutured.' She described how to isolate the anterior, lateral and posterior muscular compartments in dissection. She showed him how she had ligated the tibial, peroneal and saphenous veins, and noted that the blood pressure always rose after the peroneal artery was tied off. She transected the sural nerve above the amputation line and let it retract into the soft-tissue bed to reduce the phantom-limb sensation. With a clean scalpel she incised the dense periosteum. She gave directions in the flat, bored tone of a carpenter teaching a child to measure and cut wood, and Akhmed heard her without listening. All her Latin words and surgical jargon couldn't mitigate the helplessness he felt while watching her finish what the landmine had begun.

'Leg amputations are normal business here,' she said, and handed him the saw. He held it, expecting her to ask for it back. She looked to it and nodded. No, she couldn't be serious. She didn't expect him to do *that*, did she? She barely trusted him to fold bed sheets properly. 'You should get comfortable with this procedure as soon as possible.'

He gazed from the blade to the bone. The bone was a disconcerting shade of reddish grey; he'd expected it to be white. He had been six years old when he first realised that the drumstick he slurped the grease from was, in principle, the same as the bone that allowed him to walk, run and win after-school football matches. He hadn't eaten meat again for two years, so great and implacable was his fear that another carnivore would consume his own leg in reprisal. 'I'm not qualified for this,' he stammered.

'This is the deal,' she said calmly. She reached for his hand. That grip held more of her compassion than the past two days combined, and then it was gone, replaced by hard pragmatism, and her fingers wrapped his around the foam grip. 'This is what we do. This is what it means for you to work here.'

His hands shook and hers steadied them. The last leg surgery he had performed had been after the *zachistka*, on a boy named Akim. He had tried his best, he really had, but he couldn't be faulted for his lack of supplies and experience, for the lack of blood in the boy's body and the great abundance drenching the floor, for the bullet he didn't shoot, or for the war he had no say in; if anyone had bothered to ask his opinion, he would have happily told them that war was, generally speaking, a bad thing, to be avoided, and he would have advised them against it, because had he known that not one but two wars were coming, he would have dropped out of medical school in his first year, his reputation be damned, and gone to art school instead; had he known a domineering, cold-hearted Russian surgeon would one day ask him to cut off this poor man's leg, he would have studied still-life portraiture, landscape oil painting, sculpture and ceramics, he would have sacrificed his brief celebrity within the village, if only to safeguard himself from this man's leg.

'There's only one amputation now, but what about next time?' Sonja said. 'There could be five, ten.'

He exhaled. Sweat pasted his surgical mask to his cheeks. Sonja pushed his hand forward. The blade grated against the bone. The vibration of each thrust ran up the blade, through the handle, to his hand and into his bones. The name of the bone was *tibia* and it was connected to *fibula* and *patella*. He had studied the names that morning, but what he knew wouldn't push the saw.

'Press harder,' she instructed, steadying the bone for him. 'This isn't a delicate operation.'

Halfway through, the blade unexpectedly went red with marrow. He stopped sawing.

'What's wrong?' Sonja asked.

He could have answered that question several different ways, but he shook his head, and kept sawing. 'I didn't know human bone marrow is red. I thought it would be golden. Like a cow's.'

'The marrow of a living bone is filled with red blood cells. If we were to shake a little salt and pepper on this bone and roast it in the oven, the marrow would turn golden in about fifteen minutes,' she said.

He feared he might vomit.

'Fine work,' she said, as he sliced through the tibia. 'Just one more bone to go.'

He set the blade on the fibula and his quick hard saw-strokes spat into the air a fine white bone dust that drifted towards him, drawn by his breath, eventually dissolving into his damp surgical mask. Sonja's dark eyes leered at him in his periphery, and he pushed the saw harder, faster, wanting Sonja to see in him more than his helplessness, wanting to finish before he fainted. A dozen strokes later the foot dropped to the table. He held the remnant by the ankle, and without pause or consideration, he flipped it on its end, and blood and marrow coated his fingers as he counted six shards of glass glinting in what was left of the man's sole.

'Set that aside,' she said. 'We'll wrap it in plastic and give it to the family for burial.' She showed him how to round off the amputated bone and pad it with muscle. She pulled the posterior flap over the muscle-padded stump, trimmed the excess skin and sutured it with black surgical thread.

When they finished, he peeled off his latex gloves and massaged the pink soreness of his right palm, where the skin between his thumb and forefinger had swollen from the handle's pinch. Sonja noticed, smiled, and when she raised her right hand he wanted to be back in bed with Ula, where he could pull the covers over their heads and in the humidity of their stale breaths hold the one person who believed he was knowing, capable and strong.

Calluses covered Sonja's palm.

Chapter 5

KHASSAN GESHILOV COMPLETED THE FIRST DRAFT
of his Chechen history on the one day in January 1963 when
it didn't snow. The manuscript was 3,302 pages. When he
submitted it to the city publisher in Volchansk he was told
he needed to send it to the state publisher in Grozny, and
when he submitted it to the state publisher in Grozny he
was told he needed to send it to the national publisher in
Moscow; and when he submitted it there he was told he
needed to send *three* typed copies. Tears leaked from the
corners of his eyes as he looked at his poor, battered fingers.
But he purchased the postage, paper, typewriter ribbons and
cigarettes such a monumentally monotonous activity required,
and eighteen months later he received a phone call from the
head editor of the history section, Kirill Ivanovich Kaputzh.

'We're launching a thrilling new series called "Prehistories
of Soviet Autonomous Republics" and we would like to
publish your book as our lead title,' Kirill Ivanovich said.
Even in his surprise and excitement, Khassan asked what
the publisher meant by prehistory; the book he had written
ended in 1962. 'Prehistory,' Kirill Ivanovich explained, 'is

the time before the cultural and political presence of the Russian state.'

'But for Chechnya that would mean 1547.'

'Indeed.'

'But that's just the first chapter of my book.'

'You must be delirious in your excitement, Citizen Geshilov. That is your entire book.'

'No, that is the first two hundred and twenty-eight pages. Some three thousand follow it,' Khassan insisted. He had never imagined that the joy of being published at all and the despair of being published poorly could be tied together like opposite ends of a shoelace.

'Yes, in your joy and astonishment you have become confused. Go and celebrate your achievement, Citizen Geshilov. Accept my congratulations and best wishes. Not everyone has the opportunity to publish a two-hundred-and-twenty-eight-page book.'

And so *Origins of Chechen Civilisation: Prehistory to the Fall of the Mongol Empire* appeared the next year with little fanfare. The sole review, written for the university newspaper by one of his students, called the book 'more interesting than the average reference book'. No one wanted to read pre-Russian history books, which was precisely why Moscow was so eager to publish them. By the time Khassan reworked the remaining three thousand pages into a lopsided companion piece – burning a partial draft after pages began disappearing – Khrushchev had been deposed; in response to murky shifts of politics, Kirill Ivanovich Kaputzh, receding further into the safety of the past, decided to publish only pre-human geological surveys. They were heady days for Khassan's earth-science colleagues.

Then Brezhnev grabbed the wheel of power and captained the country with the exploratory heart of a municipal bus driver. Each passing year the publisher waded further into the morass of human history, first allowing histories of the Sumerians, then the ancient Egyptians, and by 1972, the year Ramzan was born, publishing books on the Hellenic age. Sensing the border of 1547 might be crossed within the decade, Khassan revised his tome under the title *Chechen Civilisation and Culture Under Russian Patronage*. He wrote as the voice of appeasement, justifying, glossing over, but never forgiving the four centuries of Russian depredations, believing all the while that he might slip three thousand pages of subtext past censors so sensitive to insinuation they would expurgate rain clouds from an International Workers' Day weather forecast. In a knee-height cradle, Ramzan, skullcapped and swaddled, dozed while Khassan wrote. He would never feel closer to his son than he did then, when the rustle of Ramzan's sleep accompanied the scratching of his pencil, and with one hand on the page and the other dipping into the cot he was the wire connecting this halved legacy; much later, he would remember those months when he and his boy could spend the whole day in the same room and mean nothing by the silence.

In 1974 Kirill Ivanovich provisionally accepted the book for publication, with the stipulation that two thousand pages be cut, before he was fired and briefly imprisoned for being too conservative with his edits, too vocal with his own opinions, and too Polish; eight months later, on hard labour duty some four thousand kilometres east of Poland, Kirill Ivanovich would stumble upon the artefacts of an ancient settlement while digging the foundation for a prison latrine, and would remember his assistant, a young man for whom he harboured the pangs of love that time and captivity hadn't blunted, a young man whom Kirill Ivanovich had listened to, as he read aloud passages from Khassan Geshilov's history of early civilisation, passages Kirill Ivanovich kept intact in his memory, like jars to hold and preserve the beautiful voice of his assistant. Kirill Ivanovich's successor, an editor whose aquiline nose pointed towards the prevailing political winds, decided the book required more radical revision to conform to the tedium of the era. And so began a decade of rewrites that mirrored the plummeting Brezhnev reign. The new editor stressed that the book didn't need to be more concise – if anything it should be longer, the editor said, so reviewers would dismiss its shortcomings as the price of ambition – and Khassan reupholstered the paragraphs he'd stripped under Kirill Ivanovich's guidance. He wrote tracts on nineteenth-century threshing techniques, the history of Chechen meteorology. The new editor would respond with changes so vague and inconsistent it took weeks to divine a politically safe interpretation. 'Rewrite chapter twelve as though you were not a person but a people,' one letter said. 'If you write on the fatherland, your words will face the heavens,' said another.

No longer did he write in his son's company. Ramzan had learned to speak, though Khassan wished he hadn't. The boy used his voice like a rubber mallet; *can I* was the only question that escaped his mouth, never *what* or *how* or *why*. Ramzan wasn't clever or kind or imaginative, or even overly obedient or cruel or dull, and Khassan built his aversion upon the empty cellar of what his son was not. In the historical sources there were kings and princes whose distaste for their progeny took more sadistic forms than Khassan's indifference; compared to Ivan the Terrible, he was a paradigm of good parenting. You can choose your son no more than you can choose your father, but you can choose how you will treat him, and Khassan chose to treat his as if he wasn't there. He chose to write when he should have spoken, to speak when he should have listened. He chose to read his books when he should have watched his son, to watch when he should have approached. One day when Ramzan was eight he entered Khassan's office and asked his father to teach him to ride a bicycle. 'You'll fall,' Khassan said, without looking up from the page. The moment would haunt him later. What if he had looked up?

Brezhnev appeared to be on his deathbed ten years before he finally passed, but on 10 November 1982, the country's beloved grandfather smoked his last white-filtered Novost cigarette. Brezhnev was buried in his marshal's uniform along with the two hundred medals – everything from Hero of the Soviet Union to the Lenin Prize for Literature – he had accrued in his eighteen-year tenure as General Secretary. Watching the mournful proceedings with his family (they all searched for Galina Brezhneva among the mourners to see if she would cause scandal even at her father's funeral), Khassan finally accepted the futility of his endeavour. He had travelled further than Herodotus but had written no *Histories*, had witnessed more combat than Thucydides but had written no *History of the Peloponnesian War*. His son sat on one side, his wife on the other, and they watched the tributes paid to a man whose tepid mediocrity encapsulated the era. For years he had relegated history to the past, where it was time-dulled and safe and ever-receding, but history was right there, in that moment, on the television screen, where balding and bejowled politicians paid their respects before determining the shape of the empire, where the flat, embalmed face of the beloved grandfather went translucent under the spotlights, and where finally they caught a glimpse of the daughter of the departed, her dress a scandalous pink.

Yuri Andropov replaced Brezhnev, only to die fifteen months later, and Konstantin Chernenko replaced

Andropov, only to die thirteen months after that. Again Khassan watched the funerals with his family; state funerals were the only times they came together. He couldn't have known this would be the final televised funeral of a General Secretary, but later, when remembering the gloomy cavalcade, he would imagine that the entire Soviet state was buried in Chernenko's casket. Gorbachev at least looked like he might live more than a year on the job, and soon after his ascension to General Secretary, Khassan received a call from a new, reform-minded editor, who had deposed Khassan's previous editor. The reform-minded editor had found Khassan's original manuscript from 1963 and thought it a more accurate and readable document than any of his subsequent revisions. 'All that's left is honing and updating,' the editor said. 'Now is the time. A few years ago you would have been sent to Siberia. Today you'll be lauded.'

Even the renewed fervour of his revisions couldn't keep pace with the deluge of declassified information released by state agencies. For a quarter-century his book hadn't been published because it was too accurate. Now it wouldn't be published because it wasn't, and couldn't be, accurate enough. A three-thousand-page draft took years to write. He couldn't possibly analyse and incorporate the disclosures that, on a daily basis, changed the way a Soviet historian was allowed to interpret his material. Even so, he finished a draft he was reasonably pleased with in the late summer of 1989. A few months later, when the Berlin Wall fell, not even a news agency as reliably incompetent as Pravda failed to speculate on its consequences. The reform-minded editor loved the new draft and wanted to schedule publication for the following year, but Khassan demurred. The morning headlines made the previous day's work obsolete; publishing the book now would be like building nine-tenths of a roof. The rind of buffer states diminished as republics peeled away. All of central Europe had shrugged off communist leadership, and now the Baltic states, the Black Sea states, even Moldova were discussing secession. For the first time in two millennia Chechnya had a chance at sovereignty. Everything was changing. It had to go into his book.

Everything did change, faster than his fingers could type. What he had been too cautious to hope for was pulled from his dreams and made real on the television screen. At that momentous hour on 26 December 1991, as he watched the red flag of the Union of Soviet Socialist Republics – the empire extending eleven times zones, from the Sea of Japan to the Baltic coast, encompassing more than a hundred ethnicities and two hundred languages; the collective whose security demanded the sacrifice of millions, whose Slavic stupidity had demanded the deportation of Khassan's entire homeland; that utopian mirage cooked up by cruel young men who gave their moustaches more care than their morality; that whole horrid system that told him what he could be and do and think and say and believe and love and desire and hate, the system captained by Lenin and Zinoviev and Stalin and Malenkov and Beria and Molotov and Khrushchev and Kosygin and Mikoyan and Podgorny and Brezhnev and Andropov and Chernenko and Gorbachev, all of whom but Gorbachev he hated with a scorn no author should have for his subject, a scorn genetically encoded in his blood, inherited from his ancestors with their black hair and dark skin – as he watched that flag slink down the Kremlin flagpole for the final time, left limp by the windless sky, as if even the weather wanted to impart on communism this final disgrace, he looped his arms around his wife

85

and son and he held them as the state that had denied him his life quietly died.

In the following years he lost his publisher, then his university job, then his wife, who one Tuesday morning passed away as meekly as she had lived; he didn't notice until eleven hours after her final breath. The chainsaws went silent and the forest grew back, and one war came and then another, and Khassan had his son and his book, and the prospect of finding fulfilment in either seemed as unlikely as the prospect of either surviving the decade. But Khassan still had them, and at a time when all belief dissolved, the act of possession was more important than what was possessed. The things in his life that caused him the most sorrow were the things he'd lived with the longest, and now that everything was falling they became the pillars that held him; had he a thirty-two-year-old toothache rather than a thirty-two-year-old son, he would have treasured it the same. But that, too, had its time. The unseasonably warm afternoon one year, eleven months and three days earlier, when Dokka and Ramzan returned from the Landfill – Dokka missing all ten fingers, Ramzan missing only his *pes* – was the last day Khassan had spoken to his son.

First Ramzan feigned indifference, then shouted, then pleaded for his father's conversation. How could Ramzan have known he would miss his father's monosyllabic disapproval? How could he have known that he lived in reaction to his father's expectations, needed them to know precisely the person he had failed to become?

'I'm doing this for you as much as for me,' Ramzan had said with the desperate logic of the unconvinced. 'We have a generator, electric lights, food on the table. Is it such a crime to give you insulin? To have clean drinking water?'

But Khassan, a career apologist, was fluent in the rhetoric of justification and accustomed to ignoring his son. By the fifth month his son's anger burned away, and a dense depression descended. Ramzan's footsteps filled the night. Soon painkillers and sleeping pills joined the hypodermic needles, cotton balls, alcohol swabs and insulin brought back from the military supplier. The ovular green pills left Ramzan comatose for sixteen hours, and in these spells, when the house exhaled and the floorboards went silent, Khassan entered his son's room.

On earlier excursions, he had explored the drawers, cupboard and shelves. In the upper left chest drawer he found the thirty-centimetre blade of the *kinzhal* he'd given Ramzan on his sixteenth birthday, a knife his father had given him, and his grandfather his father. Within the pages of an algebra textbook a list bore the names of those Ramzan had helped disappear. The list contained three names when he first found it neatly folded between pages 146 and 147, further into the textbook than his son had ever ventured at school. The last time he checked, a few weeks before Dokka's was to be added, twelve names were listed. But most mornings, like this one, the second morning after Dokka disappeared, Khassan had no need or desire for further incrimination. Instead he sat on the bed, and held Ramzan's hand, and spoke to him.

'I saw Akhmed this morning and he ran away from me,' Khassan said. 'He ran into the forest and hid behind a tree because I am your father.'

In these moments when his son lay encased beneath the surface of a chemically sustained slumber, when his words were extinguished like sparks released into a vacuum, Khassan spoke freely. He told stories from his youth, begged clemency for certain villagers, and once suggested Ramzan drink peppermint tea for his cough. What else could he do when honour-bound to shun his son, when disavowal was his last vestige of paternal authority? The one-sided conversations were long treks across bridges leading nowhere, but he knew no other way to span the divide; he enjoyed the spoils of the collaboration he condemned, disavowed his son for lacking the compassion he had never taught him. 'Let Akhmed be,' he whispered. 'Let the girl be. Forget their names. They are gone.'

In the chest of drawers he found the *kinzhal* sheathed unceremoniously in a vest. Three paces away, Ramzan's Adam's apple nodded like a bobber on the tide. One slice was all it would take. He had told Akhmed as much a few hours earlier. He could have taken one step, then the next, and the third. He could have lodged the butt of the handle against his breastplate and fallen forward and so taken gravity as his accomplice. There would have been blood, but he could have stomached it; a Chechen, he knew, had more blood in him than a Russian, but far less than a German. He could have, as he could have other times; but he pulled a green apple from his pocket and sliced through that instead. The core sat in two blocks of pale flesh and with the vest he wiped the juice from the blade and wished he had the fortitude to make the juice blood. What father fantasises about killing his son? Even murderers, rapists and politicians deserve fathers who separate love from repudiation, but Khassan couldn't manage that; like dye poured into water, what he felt for Ramzan was a singular, inseparable opacity. Uncomfortable with only three paces between the *kinzhal* and the neck, Khassan carried the apple outside. He sat on the shovelled back steps and whistled three times.

He surveyed the yard while waiting for the dogs to emerge from the woods. The slate grave markers and stone perimetre of the herb garden were no more than dips and rises in the snow. The garden had been his wife's suggestion, one of the few he acted on in their twenty-three years of marriage. Sharik, a pup then, had followed his nose around the yard as though pushing an invisible ball, and Khassan had planted seeds in rows marked with bent wire hangers. The dishes his wife had cooked for years soon tasted new, as though prepared by another woman, and Khassan had imagined that other woman when he made love to his wife five times that spring. Now she lay buried at the far end of the garden, beside the brown suitcase containing the bones of his parents, commemorated by a slight depression in the snow and a frozen dog turd.

Feral and matted, whittled by deprivation, the dogs loped towards the back steps. They had belonged to the neighbours his son had disappeared, and even in this state he knew them by name. They trotted through the hole he'd clipped in the fence and gathered before him in a tight semicircle, jostling and snapping at the thin slivers of apple falling from the *kinzhal* blade. He held out his hands and they licked the juice from his fingers. Like them, he was unwelcome at the homes of his neighbours and avoided on the street. Like them, he was a pariah. He nuzzled the snout of a brown mutt, reaching from the dog's muzzle to her ears, and before he knew what was happening, he was holding her as he hadn't held a human in years. The mutt − which had been a husband's tenth-anniversary gift to his wife, who had been expecting something smaller, inanimate, and in a box − licked the grease from his hair.

'You think I'm wonderful, don't you? You think I'm the kindest, bravest, most generous man ever given a pair of feet to step into the world,' he said, and the dog kept licking his hair in reply. 'That's because you're a stupid dog.'

He went to the kitchen, returned with the meat of two chickens and a lamb shank, and laid it in the snow, his hair sticky with saliva, the king and benefactor of their open maws. He would never forget his son's face the morning after Ramzan's fifth trip to the military supplier, when Ramzan opened the fridge and found nothing but condiment jars basking in the thirty-watt glow. Ramzan had stormed to the backyard, where the dogs lay on the ground, swollen stomachs pointed skyward, unable to roll, let alone stand, let alone run, and Khassan lay right there among them, his own navel aimed at the clouds, turning the dead grass into confetti, such a lovely and peculiar carelessness known only to elderly men who have napped with feral dogs. Ramzan screamed at him, picking up a thigh bone gnawed clean, pulling the gristle from the slack jaws of a blind wolfhound, and a distant happiness returned to Khassan like a word he could define but not remember. From that day, a year and a half earlier, his disapproval had expanded from silence to sabotage. If Ramzan used food to justify the disappearances, Khassan made sure it all went to the dogs. Canine affection and his son's exasperation became his only sources of pleasure. In response, Ramzan began stashing food around the house, but he soon realised that even processed meat spoiled. Then he bought a fancy fridge lock invented for fat Westerners without self-control; each morning he set aside enough for Khassan to eat that day, and locked up. But Khassan would give his three meals to the dogs and go hungry himself, and when he lost enough weight, Ramzan abandoned the tactic. Next Ramzan only bought foods to which dogs are allergic: chocolate, raisins and walnuts. But Ramzan's teeth began aching, his shit began looking like fancy Swiss confectionery, and with one glance to the insulin bottle Khassan reminded him that a diabetic couldn't live on sweets. They were wonderful days; how he enjoyed terrorising his son. In the end his boy surrendered. Couldn't outwit his father. For the past year they had communicated by the glares of a resentful truce. Khassan fed the dogs as his only family, and always left enough for Ramzan, though no more than the average villager could hope to survive on in these difficult days.

Khassan stood and smiled at the six dogs, muzzles to the ground, tails wagging languidly. One was bald, another blind. From time to time a dog would race towards the fence, chasing invisible rodents; in the vaporous insanity that had fallen across the land, even dogs hallucinated. A white shepherd dog stood at the back. He tossed him the finest cut.

'Sharik,' he said, but the dog didn't recognise his name. Three years earlier, before his son's treachery allowed them food to spare, he had let the dog go. His claws had danced frantically on the floorboards, and Khassan had had to kick twice before he scampered out the open door. For three days the dog had paced the fence, head hung, waiting for Khassan to call him back. Khassan hadn't left the house until Sharik finally had disappeared into the forest. When Ramzan had arrived with the first cardboard boxes of food, he had tried to entice the dog home, but whatever trust had existed between them was dead. Only by caring for the pack could Khassan care for his dog. That was the gift Sharik had given, and Khassan thanked him every morning with the finest cuts.

The dogs followed him round the side of the house, through weeds winter couldn't kill, to the tyre tracks furrowed in the road. They clambered behind him, trusting him as people did not, and when he unclenched his fists and wiggled his fingers, he felt cold wet noses and the warmth of their tongues.

'Did I ever tell you the story of the cobbler and his son?' he asked the brown mutt. 'Yes, you've already heard it. Sharik tells it best.'

He walked to the gap in the block where Dokka's house had stood. The dogs wouldn't follow him onto the frozen charcoal. He found the corner where Dokka's bookcase had stood, and there he bent down and scooped a handful of ash into his coat pocket. The dark dust dissolved into his palm. 'A bunch of big tough wild dogs,' he said to the pack, which waited for him on the banks of the frozen debris. 'But too afraid to follow me...' To follow him where? Where was he?

Over the road the curtained windows were two black eyes on the face of Akhmed's house. If Akhmed had left at dawn, and said he would be gone all day, who was looking in on Ula? The most painful revelations were the quietest, those moments when the map opened on the meandering path that had led him here. An ailing woman would spend the day alone; he hadn't envisioned that.

'I could call on her, see if she is all right, if she needs anything,' he said, glancing to the dogs for approval. They were all ripples on the same pond. 'If I'm looking after a bunch of dogs, the least I can do is look after her. Don't take that tone with me. I am not breaking in. I have the key right here.' He displayed the spare key Akhmed had given him with a grin, nine years earlier, on the day the bank that owned four-fifths of Akhmed's house was bombed into oblivion. The dogs cocked their heads, unconvinced. 'No, I haven't been called for, but that's beside the point. Are you sure you want to discuss etiquette? I have a lot to say about arse-sniffing as a way to say hello.'

Two paces towards the house a burgeoning worry spread through him. What if the dogs thought he was leaving them for human company? Well, he was, but he had to break it to them gently. They were sensitive souls, even if they occasionally dug up and ate newly buried bodies. He dropped to one knee and opened his arms. All but Sharik licked the aftertaste of oats from his breath, and he told them how much he loved them, how much he needed them, how he would never leave them. Then the bald dog sniffed his arse.

His highly critical canine audience observed as he knocked at the front door. 'See?' he said to them. 'I have no choice but to use the key.'

He pushed open the door and crossed the thick mustiness to the bedroom. A pair of slender legs, no more than sheet creases, shifted beneath the covers. For three minutes he watched her from the threshold, a second slice of his day spent watching a second addled mind at rest; then she rolled over. He looked into her eyes and they took their time looking back.

'You've got old, Akhmed,' she said, and he couldn't suppress his smile. Like a child, this one.

'I'm not Akhmed,' he said. Akhmed had been eight days old when they first met in the living room of Akhmed's parents in 1965. He had held the infant in his arms and a relief profound as any he would ever feel had seeped right through him. Akhmed's eight-day-old eyes had held the reflection of ten thousand possible lives. Khassan wasn't an emotive or superstitious man, and nothing like it had ever happened again, but he had found, layered in the infant's half-lidded eyes, innumerable, wanting faces, none of which he had recognised.

'I'm sorry,' Ula murmured. 'My head isn't right.'

He sat on the bed beside the bone of her hip. 'Don't apologise. I spent the morning talking to dogs.'

'If you're not Akhmed, then why are you here?'

'I wanted to see if you needed anything. If you wanted someone to talk to. Akhmed won't be back for a while.'

'He won't be back?' she seemed to ask, but he wasn't sure. She had but two notes in her, and on the wire stretching between them her questions and answers warbled the same.

'Not for a little while,' he said. Three full water glasses and a bowl of hardened rice sat on the bedside table.

Sensing his uncertainty, she again asked, 'Why are you here?'

'I miss speaking to people,' he said. When he admitted it aloud he wanted to laugh. It was that simple. He was that lonely. He had come to an invalid woman to offer the help he needed. 'I miss being able to speak. For nearly two years Akhmed has been the only person I've had a conversation with.'

'You said you spent the morning talking to dogs.'

He smiled and nodded. 'I didn't think you'd remember that. He must be the only person you've talked to in that time, too.'

'Who?'

'Do you know my name?' he asked. She strained but came back with nothing. 'That's OK,' he said. 'That's just fine.'

'Tell me a story,' she said.

'A story?'

'There were the stories of paintings. All true.'

He frowned. He didn't know the stories of any paintings. 'I only know one story,' he said. 'I can say it happened, but I can't say if it's true. Did you ever meet Akhmed's mother?' He took her empty stare for a no. 'I'm glad you remember that because you couldn't have met her. Cancer took her when Akhmed was seven. Her name was Mirza.'

She nodded because she was expected to.

'If I tell you this story, do you promise you will forget it?'

'I can't promise anything,' she said distantly. He held her wrist, felt its plodding pulse. *A mind too feeble to tell the time of day can still get the right blood to the right places,* he thought. He'd never told anyone about her. 'I will tell you about Mirza.'

He heard about the mass deportation nearly two years after it occurred, he told Ula, only after he himself had been deported to Kazakhstan. On 23 February 1944, Red Army Day, a day when Khassan had been shooting Nazis in eastern Poland, the Soviet NKVD rounded up Chechens in their town squares and forced them into Lend-Lease Studebaker trucks. Those who resisted or whom the NKVD deemed unfit for transport were shot. Packed into a coal wagon, Khassan's parents and sister slept on maize sacks and ate dry maize meal as the trains slowly steamed eastward. Local soldiers cut their hair and dusted them with delousing powder when they arrived on the Kazakh steppe. Khassan never knew what happened to his sister, only that she had been seen climbing into the coal wagon in Grozny but hadn't been seen climbing out. His parents slept in a *kolkhozniki* dormitory cellar, on a bed of dry mattress straw, and when hungry they made a flour of the mattress straw and fried thin powdery slabs that left them feverish but full. When they ran out of straw, they slept on the stone floor and made soup from grains picked from horse manure. By the time Khassan reached Kazakhstan in autumn 1945, conditions had improved but his parents had already perished, and he pieced together the story of their last year from the memories of their neighbours and friends, and from Mirza.

Mirza had been a child when Khassan left for war, and in 1947, when he came upon her straining water through cheesecloth, he didn't recognise her as the girl who, at the age of eight, had been brought up on criminal charges for drawing a charcoal moustache on her lip and goose-stepping around the barnyard, ordering livestock to become more active builders of communism. 'Let me have some,' he said, thirsty after his long way. 'Go fuck yourself,' she said simply. It was their first conversation. She would become the love of his life, but he couldn't have known that as he turned and stepped into dung so deep it reached the knot in his laces. He couldn't have known it as he prised the pail from Mirza's fingers and washed his boot in her clean water.

A year later the schoolmaster died and Khassan replaced him. He was without qualification or experience, but after the war, the squabbles of children approximated peace, and he was happy. Among his pupils was Mirza's youngest sister, a quick-witted girl, with fingernails bitten so short she couldn't lift a kopek coin from a counter, who once set a drawing pin on the chair of the commissar's chubby son to see if he would explode. Though he saved the commissar's son from the drawing pin − and thus Mirza's sister from a bullet − he recognised that thread of recklessness running through her family just asking to be snipped short.

For May Day 1950, Khassan organised a children's parade. Adults lined the stone-marked road to cheer their children and avoid the penalty of ten years' hard labour for non-attendance. Twenty-three of the ninety-six children marching that day wouldn't live to see their native Chechnya. The commissar's son would be among them because the cholera ward, without respect for political class, was the nearest to an egalitarian society that most of them would ever come. Mirza's youngest sister was one of the four who held on a raised pallet the plaster bust of Stalin. Mirza glared from across the street, her hands at her sides, the only pair there not brought together in applause. Her contempt passed through him as light through vapour. The following afternoon she confronted him in the schoolhouse with a look that would have severed weaker necks. 'You are a coward,' she said, and with that one word wrote a denunciation, a biography and a prophecy. It was their second conversation.

In 1956, three years after Stalin's death, the Chechen ethnicity was rehabilitated by the pen stroke of a distant bureaucrat. On the evening of the day the first trains arrived to transport them home, Khassan followed the pale stone road to the pale stone cemetery, carrying with him a spade and the brown suitcase his parents had last packed twelve years earlier. The earth was hard and dry, and it took several hours to reach them. His mother's index finger pointed at him through the dirt. The burial shroud had replaced their skin. They were lighter than he had expected, their muscles hard in desiccation. He folded their arms, pulled on their legs until the tendons snapped; he was as reverent as possible. He packed them tenderly within the discoloured suitcase lining. Their bones lay bowed and prostrate. He performed no ablutions, and the brown of earth and decay had rusted his hands, but God would forgive him these lesser blasphemies. They had given him as good a life as they could. He wished he could have given them a better death. He decided, then, that he would write a history of his parents, of his people, of this sliver of humanity the world seemed determined to forget. Standing in the mounded dirt the spade was a slender tombstone. He wasn't alone. Hundreds of others had come to raise and return their dead, and the dust reddened the night.

When he reached his cabin, a small shack within a perimetre of pale stone, he wanted to wash his hands. He didn't. Instead he folded the shirts he'd won in cards from

Red Army guards, the long underwear he'd stripped from a corpse, the marmot coat a Kazakh widow had traded for the promise that her departed husband's name would remain on his tongue for nine years of nightly prayers. The brown suitcase stood at the door. He had inherited no other, nothing in which to pack the clothes so neatly folded on the floor. For eleven years he had dreamed of leaving behind his folded clothes for whatever Soviet ethnicity next fell from official favour, leaving behind all but his parents' remains, and the following morning, when a locomotive whistle seared through his sleep, he awoke to that dream.

The cattle cars were filled by the time he reached the tracks. The refugees watched uncertainly as trains glided into the pale grasses of the steppe, becoming the only measure of scale. Balancing on a tie, beneath an exhaust cloud that rose like a locust swarm returning to God's mouth, he found Mirza. 'You're still here,' she said. 'I am,' he said. She lifted his brown suitcase. 'It's light,' she said. 'It's my parents,' he said. It was their third conversation.

The refugees camped along the tracks, afraid of missing the next transport, but Khassan, trusting the sky to convey the clatter of approaching trains, walked into the empty village beside Mirza. Trails of clothing, furniture and dishware flowed from the open doors of cabins and huts. The commissar and his entourage were the first to flee, and the Party headquarters, the most architecturally sound building for many kilometres, was abandoned. They passed through meeting rooms papered with bulletins announcing the repatriation, and into the commissar's office. Three upholstered chairs encircled a coffee table where a golden fountain pen stood at attention in its reservoir. Behind them, hanging over the door frame, the plaster bust of Stalin observed them coolly. Khassan lifted it from its perch — two taps to Stalin's forehead echoed in the hollow cranium – and wrapped it in a burgundy curtain. Mirza's face was unrecognisable in its approval.

Khassan carried the bust to the steppe and when he set it down the tall grasses radiated around the dead dictator's face. Mirza dropped her heel through Stalin's temple – and what could he do, when she looked at him like that, but become her accomplice? He crushed the big brown moustache, and she joined in, stamping out the left eye; their feet engaged in this fourth conversation until their boots were white with plaster dust, and they had finally committed the treason for which they had been sentenced twelve years earlier. They shrieked and whooped until their voices were hoarse and their lungs ached and the wind was carrying off the dust and it was all celebration. Finally, he spread the burgundy curtain across the grass. She reached for his cheek and he reached for her shoulder. On her stomach, to the left of her navel, an oval birthmark spread like a tipped inkwell. He placed his mouth on it.

Ula had closed her eyes, but in the quiet he felt the relief of confession like a current carrying him after he stopped kicking. It felt wonderful to be heard and forgotten. He wanted more. He wanted to erase the past he had spent his life recording. Later, in his study, he gathered his notes, rough drafts, red-line edits, everything, and set them in a bed sheet and carried them into the woods. It would take many trips, many tied bed sheets, but he would erase every word he had ever written. The dogs accompanied him, and behind them followed the memory of Mirza's accusation, now stronger, fortified by the testimony of four decades spent as a Soviet apologist. And after the fire had read his pages, and the dogs basked in the warmth, and the ashes greyed the snow, what would he write? Not a history of a nation that had destroyed history and nationhood. Something smaller. A letter to Havaa. His recollections of Dokka. He would begin with his favourite memory of Dokka, then go back to the first time he had met him, and end with Havaa's birth. It would be the first true thing he had ever written.

Chapter 6

1994 1995 1996 1997 1998 1999 2000 2001 2002 2003 **2004**

AT THAT MOMENT, HAVAA HATED THE HOSPITAL. she hated the chemicals that sharpened the air and burned her throat just like the bleach her mother used to launder sheets, when there had been bleach, and sheets, and her mother. She hated the patients, who were bruised, who were broken, who took so, so, so long to die. She hated Deshi. The nurse was old, the nurse was boring, and if she were the face of life, no wonder so many patients chose death. She frowned at the stupid yellow linoleum; what was Akhmed doing? She hated him, too. He'd thrown a lab coat over her and left her to sit by herself in the waiting room while the man hauled in on the tarpaulin filled the air with screaming and the floor with bleeding. Through the thin fabric of the lab coat, she'd watched the frantic shadows thrash about on the floor, straining to stopper everything that was pouring from that sad man. When they finished, they disappeared down the corridor, and left her there like a coat stand.

And now Akhmed had gone home, had left her again. Would he return tomorrow? Yes, he had to. She couldn't entertain other possibilities. Yes, Akhmed would return tomorrow; he would return tomorrow and he would go to Grozny, a place they always talked about going to *together*, and he would go with Sonja instead, whom he clearly liked more than her, because she was older and had breasts, and they would probably be doing something only the two of them would find fun, like inventing a way to scratch a phantom limb, and tomorrow, when he returned, she would hate him, and until then she would miss him.

A phantom limb. She still hadn't taught the one-armed guard to juggle, as she had promised Akhmed, and she hated that she wanted to impress Akhmed even when he wasn't with her. She found the guard at the hospital entrance, asleep on the bench. He wore the faded olive uniform of the rebels. She pressed her index finger into his stomach as far as it would go, which wasn't very far, because he didn't have much stomach to him. He woke with a grunt. 'What do you want?'

'To juggle.'

He closed his eyes. 'You don't need my permission. Go forth. Juggle.'

'No, I'm here to teach you to juggle.'

'You must be kidding.' He hadn't opened his eyes again.

'You aren't a one-armed freak that everyone feels sorry for,' Havaa said, as comfortingly as she could. When Akhmed had taught her to juggle six months earlier, he had used small rectangles of gauze that flapped and turned in the breeze like a shoal of starving white fish. They had stood in the middle of the street, the gusting headwind the nearest thing to traffic, the gauze strips slithering in it, and Akhmed hooting as she chased them. It had taken her all afternoon to learn to juggle one. The next day they had moved indoors. Juggling is more in your mind than your hands, Akhmed had told her; in the still air she had learned in minutes.

'Juggling is more in your mind than your hand,' she told the one-armed guard.

'I died in my sleep, didn't I? This is Hell, isn't it?'

'You begin by throwing a handkerchief up in the air,' she said, and demonstrated in an exaggerated flourish.

The one-armed guard began praying. 'Deliver me, Allah, from this cesspool of wickedness.'

'You want to make sure you cross the handkerchief, like you're pinning it to the shoulder of an invisible partner. Like a phantom partner; that should be familiar to you!'

'Jesus Christ, hear my plea,' the one-armed guard chanted, in case the infidel god was more receptive.

'Then you repeat the same movement with your other hand.'

'She thinks I have another hand.'

'See how well I can do it?' she said, all three handkerchiefs aloft.

'My phantom hand is slapping you in the face.'

'I can't feel it,' she said, proudly.

'Neither can I,' he said, glumly.

'You seem a little grumpy. Maybe you should take another nap.'

As she left the one-armed guard she hated Akhmed even more; if she couldn't tell him, it was as if she hadn't taught the one-armed guard to juggle at all. He had left her, just like her father had, and her mother, and she bandaged that wound with all the stubborn sullenness she could muster, so it would be hidden, well insulated, and so no one could see how in just three hours she had learned to miss him with the same incredible longing she reserved for her parents. She should have known Akhmed would forget her as quickly as he had her mother.

She didn't hate Sonja, not as much as Akhmed. Sure,

Sonja was curt and short-tempered, a humourlessist incapable of finding in an hour the fun Akhmed could conjure in a minute. But that was OK because Sonja was different. Sonja was the boss of this place, ordering everyone around, and even Akhmed went pale when she spoke. Not only was Sonja a doctor, she was the head of the entire hospital. Women weren't supposed to be doctors; they weren't capable of the work, the schooling, the time and commitment, not when they had houses to clean, and children to care for, and dinners to prepare, and husbands to please. But Sonja was more freakish, more wondrously confounding than the one-armed guard; rather than limbs she had, somehow, amputated expectations. She *didn't* have a husband, or children, or a house to clean and care for. She *was* capable of the work, school, time, commitment and everything else it took to run a hospital. So even if Sonja was curt and short-tempered, Havaa could forgive her these shortcomings, which were shortcomings only in that they were the opposite of what a woman was supposed to be. The thick, stern shell hid the defiance that was Sonja's life. Havaa liked that.

And so she wandered along the corridor, wondering what she might be like if she lived like Sonja. Maybe she could be an arborist, like her father. She hadn't thought that women were allowed to be scientists, but if Sonja could be a surgeon and hospital head, why couldn't she be an arborist? Or a sea anemonist? She slowed to peek into the room where the legless man slept. Blood dried darkly on his bandages. His stump poked from the edge of the white bed sheet like a rotten log through snow cover. He slept. Somewhere in that hazy, heroin-induced slumber, he was already designing in dreams the monument to war dead he would, in twenty-three years, make of steel and concrete.

He was the only person in the hospital right now she didn't hate.

'I thought I told her to find something to do,' Deshi said, entering the room with her customary frown.

'I was.'

' "I was," she says. Was what?'

'Thinking,' Havaa shot out, like a pebble cast towards the nurse's flat face.

'Find something more useful to do,' Deshi said. She knitted as she leaned against the wall. The yarn ball slowly rolled in her pocket.

'Does Sonja order you around like this?'

'Why would she say that?'

'Because Sonja runs the hospital.'

'Unbelievable,' Deshi said with a sigh. 'I've been working here since before Sonja was a kick in her mother's stomach, was already retired when I hired her, and she gets the credit for making this place run. They'll take everything from you, even the respect of an orphan girl with too many questions in her mouth.'

'Why is the hospital run by women? What happened to all the men?'

'They ran away.'

'But they're the brave ones.'

'No, they're the ones that break your heart and leave you for a younger woman.'

'So you're saying that sometimes women are braver than men. And better doctors.'

'I'm saying that if you want to keep a man, you better hide his shoes every night so he can't walk out on you.'

'I don't understand.'

Deshi shook her head. Her romantic advice was worth a foreigner's ransom, and here she was, giving it freely to a girl who couldn't appreciate the hard-earned wisdom. 'Just stay away from oncologists, OK?' she said, and led the girl to the waiting room. 'If you just remember that, you'll spare yourself the worst of it. Now, why don't you get your notebook out and draw something?'

'Like what?'

'I don't know. Where would you most want to be right now?'

'My home,' she said. She thought the word meant only the four walls and roof that held her, but it spread out, filled in, Akhmed, the village, her parents, the forest, everything that wasn't here. 'A week ago.'

'And I'd rather be right here forty years ago, when they first offered me the job. I'd wag my finger right in the head nurse's face and say, no, no, you won't trick me, and I'd walk right out those doors.'

'It's stupid. There are maps to show you how to get to the place where you want to be but no maps that show you how to get to the time when you want to be.'

'Why don't you draw that map?'

'Only if you let me play on the fourth floor.'

'Child, if there was such a map, there would still be a fourth floor. Start drawing.'

The sharp, chemical-curtained corridor swallowed Deshi's footsteps and Havaa was alone again. The notebook tilting on her legs, she thought of her father. She didn't hate him. Thinking that, realising it, feeling it crackle through her arm bones, her finger bones, feeling her arms wrapping around her chest, her fingers clasping her shoulders, this trembling inside her that was only the beat of her heart. Each night he would tell her tales about an alien green-bodied race whose faces consisted of a singular orifice through which they saw, ate, smelled, heard, thought and